STEALING THE SILVER FOX

DANIEL MAY

Copyright © 2023 by Daniel May

All rights reserved.

No part of this book may be reproduced in any form or by any electronic or mechanical means, including information storage and retrieval systems, without written permission from the author, except for the use of brief quotations in a book review.

BLURB

Ezra Fontaine, a cutthroat CEO and divorcé, whose only soft spot is for his luxury car collection.

Anton 'Tony' Cargill, a proud slacker and greasemonkey, who develops a work ethic for the first time in his life when he gets his hands on his richest (and finest) customer's private number.

After a spontaneous string of drunken texts, Tony's 'natural gifts' have Fontaine on the hook. But landing the silver fox won't be as simple as just whipping it out.

Or will it?

Stealing the Silver Fox is a high heat, reverse age gap (younger top) MM romance which takes place in the same universe as *Claiming the Cleanfreak* and the *Fresh Taste of Ink* series.

CONTENT WARNING

Stealing the Silver Fox contains a thirty year age gap (all characters are over 18 and legal adults), underage drinking, some drug use (marijuana, implied others), and demeaning language and sexual acts. But that's probably why you're here, isn't it?

1 SNVC MAGNOLIA

Tony knew nothing about Ezra C. Fontaine except the stuff that really mattered: he was divorced, he was keeping it *tight* at fifty-two (in what was probably a big, spiteful 'fuck you' to his ex-husband), and he had a long, fat cock.

Of course Tony had not *seen* his cock.

He'd only glimpsed its outline through the crisp cut of Fontaine's suit.

And it had taken *weeks* of persistent, hawklike attention to catch *just* enough of that outline to draw a sure conclusion.

Fontaine did not wear crude, tight pants or freeball it. Not even to visit the mechanic. No, he always stopped by on his way to or from the office, immaculately suited in a way that made Tony want to sink his teeth into the upholstery of whatever car he was servicing at the time.

Tony had caught his good glimpse just that once, coming in from a smoke break at the right moment on the right day.

Fontaine had been speaking to Tony's boss's boss with a frown on his face. He had been in midstride. His pants had been light in color, the sunlight striking his groin just right. And Tony had gotten a second's perfect silhouette of CEO cock.

A cock long and fat enough to make Tony's tonsils all cozy like two friends joined by a third, huddling close together beside a winter fire.

That had been Tony's first evening of overtime.

He had hung back to "—finish some stuff up," waving his hand to say "Nah, you guys go on ahead, I'll meet you at the bar later."

And he would.

Once he had committed that chunky bulge to spank bank immortality.

As soon as the garage was empty, Anton Cargill had flung himself behind the wheel of Fontaine's fancy, navy blue 1974 SNVC Magnolia, and jerked himself silly.

Tony's creativity began and ended with what his dick decided was interesting. The same mind which had produced *'Jim Noseman's Big Day Out'* in creative writing class — a blatant ripoff of *Ferris Bueller's Day Off*, but featuring a giant nose for a protagonist — and passed by the skin of his teeth largely because the teacher desperately wanted him gone, went into overdrive contemplating Ezra Fontaine.

Green-grey eyes. Merciless gunslinger eyes, sheriff's eyes, *'this town ain't big enough for the both of us,'* eyes. The thousand-yard middle distance stare as he ignored them all, gazing out at the sun-white windows by the front desk as if he could see some fantastical plane that they could not... and that he was not impressed by.

Great eyes.

...Great pecs.

Big, firm ba-habba-wabbas. Stress balls. Hooters. Bazongas.

And there was more.

Firm round peach of an ass that looked downright indecent in his bespoke suits.

Big hands. Rough-looking knuckles. Light skim of hair on his arms, in the rare moments Tony glimpsed him with sleeves pushed up.

A thick neck and set of broad shoulders that suggested a bull, and made Tony want to say 'yee haw!' and bulldog him bareback into the dirt.

Tony imagined all of that, sprawled in the crisp leather interior of the back seat. Fontaine's belt opened, pants dragged roughly down to his feet. The black smudges of greasemonkey hands holding him down by the waist. Tony's mouth big-O swallowing him whole, and then bobbing up and down and in and out, deepthroating him good and sloppy and noisy. A proper *'gluk gluk gluk.'*

Those big hands clutching in Tony's kitchen-sink, scissors-cut, not-quite mullet like a big-titted broad getting eaten out in a porno.

And speaking of big-titted.

He imagined shoving the big, muscle-thick silver fox's shirt up, over the swells of his chest, baring his pecs to the sunroof of his Magnolia, fat and round and firm, and taking a squeezy handful, just as Tony took a squeezy handful of himself now, saying "*Heughh*," and coming all over the steering wheel.

Tony cleaned up the steering wheel, then spit-shone the rest of the garage to give a plausible excuse for his lingering late and alone.

This got to be routine.

Tony had never been a better employee.

He was clocking in loads of overtime, and his boss — who had been all but gun-to-head forced to hire Tony, and never a fan — had never been happier.

The big-bellied, cigar-crunching Mayhew — an ex biker who had never learned to turn it off — actually clapped Tony on the shoulder one morning when he came in. Tony jumped guiltily, thinking the boss man checked some unknown security camera and caught him at it.

Nope. "Look for a little extra in your next paycheck," said Mayhew, with that touch of the patronizing in his voice, which shit bosses got sometimes when they thought they were responsible for a sudden change in an employee's spirit. "Whatever's gotten into you, I'd like to see more of it."

"Right, sure, yeah," said Tony eloquently, and skittered off to his station to pretend to work for another seven hours.

Fontaine was coming in that day; a pebble had bounced off of his raspberry colored Kimura Cloud and left a dent. Unacceptable.

Tony awaited the exec's arrival with a horned-up anxiety that kept him at half mast all morning.

Of course, when Fontaine finally showed up, it was when Tony had just stepped out for a piss, but he didn't miss much.

When Tony emerged, wiping his wet palms on his mechanic's-filthy shirt — their bathroom out of paper towels, as usual, while the client bathroom was fully stocked with mints and hand towels — he heard Fontaine before he saw him.

Ezra Fontaine didn't *yell*. He didn't bark like a drill sergeant. And he didn't curse.

He didn't have to.

He spoke with absolute clarity — each word a separate boot to the ribs, stomping the shit out of his verbal target — and loud enough to be heard in the back of any boardroom.

Especially because, when Ezra Fontaine spoke, everyone shut the fuck up.

Tony joined the mechanics and other greasemonkeys by the garage doors, where they were all enjoying the spectacle of Fontaine demolishing the latest secretary.

"She tried to bump his appointment," said one of them gleefully.

They didn't have anything against the new girl, but Fontaine was a spectacle to be saluted, even if you weren't drooling all over yourself to fuck him.

But Tony *was* drooling all over himself to fuck him.

He didn't hear a word coming out of the man's mouth; his mind was full of that hard, cold profile, and the frowning lips, and the thought of stuffing those lips with cock.

Bending Fontaine over his Kimura Cloud, pants around his ankles, balls deep clap-clap-clapping his cheeks red, scraping up the perfect raspberry paint job.

Getting Fontaine on his knees, pulling him by the silver hair so his face was nestled into Tony's balls, feeling the exciting, shivery bristle of that immaculately trimmed beard and the slick, hot, wet mouth and tongue.

"—know Perry's schedule, right?"

"Wha-huh?" said Tony, blinking and looking around.

He had been called upon. The others shoved him towards the front desk, where the secretary pleaded with her eyes.

Tony drifted forward, hands thrust in overalls pockets. A long, tall stretch of nineteen-year-old.

"Whuh?"

He did not look at Fontaine, who did not look at him, either. To be a greasemonkey was to go thrillingly unseen.

The secretary leaned towards Tony, speaking in a hushed voice as if they could conceal anything from the man standing right there. "Do you know what time Perry gets in?"

"Um." Tony mulled. He ran his hand through his hair, pretending to stare thinking into space, space which was conveniently located right around the territory of Fontaine's fly. He imagined undoing it with his mouth. "What day is it?"

"*Tony.*" She despaired. "It's *Tuesday.*"

"Then..." Tony shrugged, rubbed his scrubby-stubbly chin. "Sometime between eight and ten?"

"But it's *eleven.*" She looked like she might cry.

Mayhew saved the moment, emerging from his office with a bark of "What's the problem?"

The other goombahs quickly scattered back to their work, but Tony — who had been *summoned* and therefore was *involved* — stood there very happily like furniture, completely ignored.

The trio found space for Fontaine's big raspberry Cloud on the schedule, and the man cooled. Though he had barely raised his voice, the atmosphere tangibly relaxed when Fontaine decided he was no longer interested in being angry.

"I can pick it up between six and eight-thirty tomorrow," he said briskly. There was no question of whether or not the car would be ready by then. He drummed his fingers once on the counter; it was the only outward sign of his impatience. The motion both drew Tony's eyes and provoked a downstairs situation, as his mind supplied a mental image of those fingers wrapped obediently around his dick. "Will there be someone here to handle keys?"

"Tony will be here," said Mayhew immediately. "Right, kid?"

As they remembered his existence, Tony took a two-inch sidestep, ensuring his lump was concealed by the counter.

"Sure," he said placidly, and nothing else.

"He'll take care of you," promised Mayhew.

Sure *would* take care of him, thought Tony in a distant, horny fog. Rip those pants right off, put Fontaine's legs up around his ears, and suck his taint like a Sour Patch Kid. Thumb-pop his prostate until he was jetting all over his stomach. Fuck him until there was a permanent mark, the exact shape of Tony's balls, pounded to a bruise over his tailbone.

"Fine." Fontaine was digging in his wallet — pricey, glossy leather — and drawing out a card, which he slid over to the secretary. "I have a new, *private* number." He pinned his eyes on Mayhew. "If I get one more call from your employees trying to pitch me a business, I'm taking *mine* elsewhere."

"Of course." Mayhew didn't blink; he was shameless, and so were the monkeys he hired. "No problem."

Yeah.

Tony eyeballed the card.

No problem.

2 ROSEMARY AND LEMON ZEST

The difference between the two men — well, one man, one nineteen-year-old who could pass for thirty thanks to muscle and really superb stubble genes — was dramatic, even now that Tony had slipped out of his garage-blackened overalls and into a perfectly respectable button-up and dark jeans. Mostly unscuffed.

Tony still had a hint of the ever-present grime under his fingernails, while his cousin's were immaculately manicured. Tony's hair, though washed, was still a wild almost-mullet, curling at the nape of his neck and poofing gloriously over his forehead. His cousin was a vision of c-suite exec sleekness complete with pristine, hundred dollar haircut, twenty-thousand timepiece glistening on his wrist, and an air of 'I'm better than this' where 'this' referred to both the interaction with his cousin and the rooftop gelato shop where they had agreed to meet.

Anton 'Tony' Cargill did not have much in common with Zachary Goff except the characteristic family dimples and a ruthless streak.

But blood was blood, and here they sat. Negotiating.

Goff was first at bat.

"When are you going to give up that joke you call a job," he asked, "and take a cozy internship like the rest of the family?"

The rest of the family.

As far as Tony was concerned, he had left 'family' behind after the *roarer* of a fight with mommy and daddy. Exactly what the fight had been about, he could barely remember; maybe it had not been so much one fight as it had been the culmination of every other fight between born-rich parents (both artists, one overmedicated, one under) and a kid who felt he had missed his destiny when the hair metal boat sailed decades ago.

Tony's split from them and their purse strings had involved a screaming match, and him shredding his mom's ten thousand dollar vintage handbag in the fireplace.

After that pivotal moment, Tony had decided he would rather live in his car and seek out 'like, the real world, *dad*,' than follow either parent to a fine arts degree.

He had chosen the bohemian life.

(He definitely hadn't been booted out on his ear while his mom went into hysterics over her bag.)

However, after a few months of showering at a Planet Fitness and bumming cigarettes from strippers — who worked at a joint across the street from his usual parking spot, and had taken him on as a kind of sad, cute, gangly mascot, occasionally buying him the big breakfast deal at the corner diner — Tony had been delighted to embrace 'family' again when Zachary Goff materialized.

Exactly how or why Goff had tracked him down remained a mystery which Tony felt no desire to poke with a stick. They had barely so much as bumped elbows at a family reunion before. Tony could only assume that the generosity had to do with Goff's own self image, and a kind of *itchiness* at knowing that someone even tangentially related to him was slumming it.

Tony didn't trust his cousin (who had definitely murdered his father, by the way, and everyone knew it) one bit, but he wasn't going to look a gift free apartment in the mouth.

Goff had put him up in one of many high rises the family brand owned, under the condition that Tony get a job.

But apprentice greasemonkeying was apparently not the kind of job Goff had had in mind.

"I don't want to sit in meetings all day talking about synergy and workflow," said Tony. "I like cars."

"Is that what you think I do all day?" asked Goff. "Sit in meetings, talk about synergy and workflow?"

Tony immediately had a mental image of knees busted with tire irons, feet drying in concrete shoes, mysterious barrels tossed into the ocean, and lied, "Something like that. Anyway, I've found my niche."

And he bit decisively into his ice cream.

He tried not to make a face.

The upscale gelato joint had only exotic flavors — and not *fun* exotic, but exotic like activated charcoal, mung bean, and peppercorn.

Tony's was rosemary and lemon zest.

The shop sat perched on the roof of a downtown building, one of only a handful that predated the surrounding skyscrapers. Below was a cafe populated only by the kind of well-suited, type A executives that Goff treated like quarry. The kind of executives whose ranks he kept exhorting *Tony* to join.

"Your niche," repeated Goff.

He sat across from Tony, lounging slightly askance like a mafia don. He held his own ice cream cone without eating it, regarding Tony with the familial combination of contempt and amusement.

"What niche is that?" asked Goff. "Scrubbing bits of dead hookers out of high end foreign cars? Learning fun new swear words from men who couldn't hack the real world and dropped out of high school? Upselling rose-gold rims to sugar babies?"

The vitriol in his voice was not surprising, but Tony shifted uncomfortably anyway. Wanting to defend what he had come to think of as 'the guys' but wanting even *more* not to get kicked out of the cozy pad Goff had set him up in.

Tony knew his cousin was a snake.

Knew that Goff had an agenda in letting him crash, knew that each free meal, ice cream treat, and night under that roof was digging him in deeper.

But Tony was blessed with the mental cushion of the young, big-dicked, and carefree, a kind of halo which colored the world around him with optimism. The chutzpah that said confidently 'all will be fine, and you will get your dick sucked, pronto, by someone, somewhere.'

"I like it there," he said. He shrugged. "They like me. They gave me a nickname."

"Do I even want to know?" asked Goff. His disdain showed for a rare moment on his face, lip lifting maybe a millimeter.

"Spider Monkey," said Tony. "Because we both have long arms." He stretched his out as if to say 'See?'

Then Goff did make a face. He glanced around, as if hoping none of his c- and v-suite peers would have a hankering for gelato that day and spot him sitting with 'Spider Monkey.'

"You can't crash on my couch forever," he said. "And that greasy little sweatshop won't maintain your current standard of living. I don't see 'assistant automotive tech' offering a lot of upward mobility."

...he was right about the second part.

On the other hand, Tony thought that 'crashing on his couch' was a generous way of putting it. He hadn't once seen Goff at the apartment — which had been as huge, ice cold, and completely empty as an art gallery when Tony first arrived — and suspected his cousin didn't even know *which* penthouse he'd stashed Tony in.

"We could make a deal," he suggested, thinking to more waylay his cousin than actually *commit* to anything. He took another bite out of his rosemary and lemon zest gelato.

He had said the magic words; Zachary Goff *liked* making deals.

Goff didn't move, but he developed a small, ominous smile.

"Let's hear it," he said.

Tony thought he had just the right material to force a stalemate. Something even *Zachary Goff* couldn't get him. An unwinnable prize.

"There's this guy I'm into," he said, playing it up, going all puppy-dog eyes. "But I can't get him to look twice at me."

"*You?*" Goff's dry voice was only half-mocking; he was aware of Tony's propensity for working his way through a population of DILFs like an invasive predator. "Say it isn't so. Have you tried subtly banging out a set of clap push-ups when he walks by?"

"He's not my usual type," said Tony. Here 'usual type' meant soccer coach, best friend's dad, sister's boyfriend's dad, much older tutor his parents had hired to try and fix his GPA, the works. "He's more... your type."

"My type?" Goff raised one eyebrow.

"Like your *type*," said Tony, gesturing up and down at the bespoke suit, twenty-k watch, the all-of-it. "He's all class. Works on Woodrose and everything."

"Works on Woodrose, eh?" Goff reflected. It was their city's version of Wall Street. "What's his name?" There was a thoughtful glint in his eye.

If Tony had been quicker on the draw, he might have thought better of name-dropping his crush to this particular cousin.

But he was not, and did not.

"Ezra," he said, and paused, drawing it out for the drama. "...Fontaine."

Goff stared at him for a moment.

Then Zachary Goff burst into peals of uncharacteristic laughter. He had to put down his still uneaten ice cream, wiping the teary corner of his eyes.

"*That* dinosaur?" he asked. He picked up his phone and began scrolling through it, looking for something. "The town pump? Ezra Fontaine? As in 'EZ' Ezra, *that* Ezra Fontaine?"

He didn't even wait for Tony to respond before pulling up whatever he'd been searching for, turning his phone around to show him a picture.

Tony took the phone and squinted at it.

For a moment the picture resembled some kind of art piece like his mom would have done. One of the abstract photos of misshapen peppers, shot in black and white for maximum focus on their glossy skin and nearly human curves.

Except that these weren't *nearly* human curves, he realized. They *were* human curves.

It was a picture of a man, naked except for a pair of snug black boxer briefs, bound with rope in dim lighting in what might have been a closet. The lighting was dim, the man in shadow, but Tony could see enough to know that he had been tied with his thighs open and knees bent, ankles tied to thighs so his legs were forced to stay spread. His hands were bound behind his back.

There was a sleep mask type of blindfold on, and a strip of tape over the mouth.

Without the suit and icy stare, Ezra Fontaine might have been unrecognizable to anyone else, but Tony *knew* that silver hair. He had fantasized too many times about twisting his fingers in it not to know it on sight.

Tony disregarded his half-eaten ice cream with a *thunk* in a trash can adjacent to their table, not looking up from the picture.

"How did you get this?"

"How do you think?" asked Goff, transparently enjoying the shock on Tony's face. "What do you think the 'EZ' in Ezra stands for?"

Tony wasn't stupid. He was, in fact, clever, in the limited ways his cushy upbringing had let slip through the cracks.

But he was very distracted by the picture. Blood had abandoned the logical parts of his brain. In fact, abandoned his brain altogether.

"*You* fucked him?" he blurted out.

The idea didn't even make him jealous, it was too dumbfounding.

"Who didn't?" Goff shrugged and discarded his own gelato cone. "He was a mess after he split with his husband, giving it up left and right.

I'm surprised he still shows his face on Woodrose after so many people have bukkaked it."

Tony's mouth was suddenly wet.

It moved without real thought, blurting out:

"What was he like?"

Goff paused. His eyes moved up and off to the side, reflecting. Tony could practically see his mind traveling backwards in time, sliding a thin tome of memory off some internal shelf and opening it, examining its contents.

Then Goff smiled in a very odd way. "Sloppy," he said. "Desperate." His voice was definitive, but almost clinical in its neutrality. Almost like a doctor recalling a particular patient. "Ezra had a complex about being denigrated. You could spit on him, slap his face, step on his balls. He liked all of it."

The recollection looked fond. Did not *feel* fond. Felt *nasty*.

But it wasn't enough to keep Tony (or his eagerly anticipatory dick) down.

He licked his suddenly dry-feeling lips and looked at the picture again; Goff still had not asked for his phone back.

The lighting was unhelpful, but Tony thought he saw *marks*.

Bruises on the backs of the thighs, mostly obscured by the position Fontaine was tied in. Maybe on the back... just past the hunched mound of his shoulders. Belt marks?

God, he was fit. Tony imagined him in the gym. Sweating. Imagined licking the sweat off.

"So, what is it?" asked Goff, examining Tony's transfixed expression. Amused. "You want an introduction? You want advice?"

Tony, who had been prepared to knock this out of the park, floundered. He hadn't expected his cousin to actually *know* Fontaine, let alone know that he liked having his *balls* stepped on.

His eyelids fluttered, distracted. The mental image of Ezra Fontaine, bound, thighs spread, still hung in front of his eyes.

"Uh..." he said. "...yeah?"

"And in exchange you'll take a job with a little more dignity, a little less elbow grease, and get the hell out of my apartment?"

"Hang on." Tony tuned back in, gaze sharpening on his cousin, realizing he was being hypnotized. "Not *just* for advice or an introduction."

"Right," said Goff. "You want to get your dick wet."

He plucked his phone back, smiling. It was a kind-*looking* smile, but it was not kind.

"I'll help you get your grubby mitts on Ezra Fontaine," he said. "But you have to keep hold of the leash on your own — like a grown up. If you lose him I'm not getting you another one, or letting you out of the deal. Think you're up to it?"

Tony scoffed aloud in a way that said *'I've handled worse.'* "Piece of cake," he said.

But he felt sweat beading up on the back of his neck. Right under the curls of his haphazard, kitchen-scissors DIY mullet.

He pushed his fingers through his hair and played it cool, projecting his cousin's semi-psychopathic chill.

"Hey, can you send me that pic?"

"Get your own."

3 THE DRAGON

Tony's apartment (okay, Zachary's, sue him) overlooked and had a great view of the park — not that Tony ever looked at it. The place was big, open, with floor to ceiling windows just about everywhere. When you lived in a fish bowl like that, you stopped paying too much attention to what was going on outside.

Through a private entrance, past a friendly doorman, up an elevator, and punching in the code to his door, Tony tossed his crazy key ring — heavy with the handfuls of discards and lost keys he'd collected at work — into its bowl and went whistling about the place.

Luxury and squalor.

That was the name of the game when you were nineteen, fat off the silver spoon, cut off from your trust fund and your pissed-off family's money, working in a garage making a few bucks above minimum wage, playing fast and loose with your sky's-the-limit credit cards, and couch-crashing with a cousin so loaded he'd probably forgotten *which* apartment he'd let Tony make his own.

And *oh*, had Tony made it his own.

Space virtually denuded of normal furniture. Punching bag hanging from the high ceiling. Weight rack and bench sitting out in the open, dominating the space. A single couch — high end, Corinthian leather, for chill and fucking on. A scratched-to-shit coffee table he and a friend had hauled in from a curb, its surface littered with 420 paraphernalia, Cheeto crumbs, empty or half empty bottles of bud, and marked like a lunar landscape with the full and half circles of water rings. Hashtag no coaster life.

His drug dealer and best friend, Jonah Squires, was currently doing pull-ups on the bar installed in the kitchen doorway, grunting on each count. He was wearing workout shorts, white crew socks, and that was it. All the better to show off his sixpack and twin 'tribal' tattoo sleeves which, of course, had to be on display at all times.

"Nine," Jonah huffed, hefting himself up as Tony approached, not acknowledging him. "Ten. Eleven."

Tony punched him in his gut by way of greeting. Jonah grunted in response but did not let go; he had already flexed his abs in defense, absorbing the blow.

It was a routine hello from them for them.

Tony ducked past him and into the kitchen. The marble island was another wasteland of the lifestyle, covered in debris. Empty cans. Empty bottles. Haphazardly closed bags of chips, discarded plastic takeout cutlery, red solo cups and a few withering, thoroughly abused limes.

Tony popped open the fridge and perused.

A two liter of mixed screwdriver ready to go. Margarita mix. Several tubs of Greek yogurt. Protein shakes.

No beer. They'd gone through all of that over the weekend.

He lifted the lid of a pizza box to find the leftovers growing moss.

Behind him, Jonah huffed a final "Fifteen," then dropped from the bar, muscles popping and lightly shiny from sweat.

"Well aren't *you* a fancy boy," he remarked, observing Tony's cleancut 'meeting the cousin' getup. "What are we all dressed up for?"

Tony grabbed a bottle of water — Penguin brand, charcoal filtered, imported from the Swiss Alps — from the fridge door and took a swig, leaving the door open. "Meeting my psychopath cousin. He wants me out."

"That sucks, man." Jonah tsked sympathetically, reached into the fridge, and did the exact same gesture of lifting the pizza box lid and dropping it in disappointment. He grabbed a water bottle of his own and chugged it all in one go, so hard and fast the plastic crunched. Wiping his mouth, he asked, "Why?"

Tony watched Jonah toss the crumpled bottle carelessly into the heaping sink, in the half where they piled their recycling.

Why, indeed.

But fuck it.

Tony didn't answer the 'why?'

Instead, he chugged the last of his Penguin water and tossed his bottle in with the others, miming a basketball layup. The heap of plastic rattled, threatening to spill out over the counter and onto the floor.

"Wanna fuck this place up?" he suggested.

Jonah grinned.

Jonah wasn't so much Tony's dealer as he was the 'connection,' because Jonah was a fucking gourmand. Tony didn't care what he was putting in his body as long as it worked and didn't kill him. Jonah, on the other hand, could talk for hours about strains of weed, shroom growing techniques, research chemicals, you name it. So Tony outsourced the getting of goods to him.

Jonah was equally responsible for sourcing the 'talent.'

Talent was important. You had to have the right people when you threw a party; wild enough to throw some curveballs at the evening, not wild enough that you had to call an ambulance.

Jonah had filled the place right up, and Tony sat on his nice couch in front of his trashed coffee table with music throbbing in the background, mood light strobing darkly through the good-sized throng of people, a good buzz on and strengthening as he vented to the girl sitting next to him.

"—wants me in the family business," Tony was saying, gesticulating with glass in hand, just on the edge of spilling it. "Toeing the family line, just like him. Look and dress... *just like him*."

"Like in the suit?" His new friend — Zelda, a ginger with black lipstick and a half dozen piercings — helped him balance his drink, guiding his hand back to the table. "And the tie? Gross. Vom."

"Yeah," said Tony, mind drifting to other things. That picture. "Suit and tie."

Jonah tossed himself down on the couch out of nowhere, still shirtless, still proudly sporting not much but ink and a 'SHELLFISH ALLERGY' medical bracelet.

"What's he going to do?" blabbed Jonah — very sloshed, pupils huge — joining in as if he had been a part of the conversation the whole time. "Call security to kick you out? Call the cops?" He mimed putting a phone to his ear, putting on a whiny affect. "'Hey, officer, my cousin is still crashing on my couch when he *pwomised* he would leave, can you come tase him? Hello? *Hellooo?*"

He put his pretend phone down, scoffed, and then pulled a joint out from behind his ear like a magic trick. He waggled it temptingly in the air. Then in a normal voice, lighting up, he added, "And cause all that family drama? Doubt it!"

"The last guy he booted out," said Tony, feeling very relaxed, very chill, taking the joint as Jonah passed it, "got a gun stuck in his mouth. Ended up under a bridge."

There was a pause as he puffed, and then all three of them busted up laughing.

It was a good night.

Zelda read their palms. Jonah danced on the table. Some guy showed off his pet tarantula. Tony drank something that glowed in the dark out of a test tube.

The party ebbed to a few stragglers, and after making a whole circuit of the apartment and coming back without his shirt, Tony ended up on the couch again.

Looking at his phone.

Looking at a number saved as a note, not as a contact.

Tony hadn't had the balls to make it a contact.

Zelda crashed down next to him, putting her big black boots up on the table with the comfort of someone who had gone from stranger to BFF in one night. The magic of intoxicants.

"Whatcha looking at?" she asked. Her lipstick was smeared; Jonah was wearing half of it.

"I stole his number," said Tony.

"Whose number?" asked Zelda.

"Yeah, whose number?" echoed Jonah, again materializing out of nowhere and joining in as if he'd been at their sides the whole time. Someone had drawn hearts around his nipples in black lipstick.

"The silver fox," said Tony.

By the time the party waned, most of the guests having meandered peacefully out, Jonah had passed out on the coffee table and Zelda was riffling through a set of Tarot cards.

"Do you want some life advice?" she asked from the floor.

"From you?" asked Tony. He sat on the couch with a sense of mild vertigo spinning pleasantly around him, not quite sure at this point if the source was booze, weed, or *other*. There had definitely been something weird in the hookah.

"From the *cards*," said Zelda, flashing them between her fingers, looking like a high stakes poker dealer.

"Yeah," said Tony. "Yeah, I do."

"I'm going to give you a one card spread," she said. "We'll ask the deck a simple question and let a single card determine the answer."

"Okay," he said, sliding off the couch to sit across from her, nodding his head. He kept nodding his head; the vertigo felt nice. He didn't feel like he was sitting on the floor at all. He wasn't sitting on anything. "Okay, okay."

She formed the deck from a ripple back into a whole, fanned out the cards, and said, "We're going to ask the deck for guidance at this point in your life, what you need to resolve your current situation."

"Okay," he said, still nodding.

She offered the cards to him.

"All right, now pick one and put it face-down."

He reached out — the air felt like jelly around his weak fingers — and plucked one from its fellows, obediently placing it face-down on the floor. The back of the card was green and gold. Patterns of leaves, no lettering.

Zelda turned the card over.

A face stared up at Tony — a purplish-black serpent's face, one rising out of shadows. There was a glimpse of a long, muscular neck bedecked with spines, spines like the ones that rose around its face like a crown.

A banner crossed the bottom of the card, reading: THE DRAGON.

He furrowed his brow down at it.

Zelda oohed, impressed. "Good one, good one," she said, giving a little clap, as if he had picked it out by skill. "We love the dragon."

"Is this a real tarot deck?" he asked suspiciously.

"The dragon," said Zelda, ignoring his question, "is the master of all things. His dominion over the natural world extends into the world of man via our concealed, *repressed* animal natures."

Tony crossed his arms over his chest. Brow still furrowed, lips pursed, he squinted down at the dragon.

It had twin golden slits for eyes.

"Where are its wings?" he asked.

Ignoring him still, Zelda went on, "The dragon signifies your hidden power."

"My hidden power?" Tony looked up, forgetting his questions, lighting up.

Zelda nodded her ginger head solemnly. "If you search within yourself," she said, "and honor your instincts, you will find the dragon's strength. It is *your* strength."

"*My* strength," he repeated, mesmerized.

"This," said Zelda, tapping the card, "is your answer."

Tony couldn't even remember the question.

What had been *in* that hookah?

He picked up the card. The dragon swam before his eyes, menacing with its golden squint and frill of sharp spines. It didn't look mythological; it looked prehistoric, like some kind of dinosaur.

"The dragon," he whispered.

"Hey, can I crash on your couch?" asked Zelda, now scrolling through her phone. "My roommate is mad I sent her a picture of Kermit with boobs and locked me out of the apartment."

"Sure," said Tony, not listening, not looking up.

The dragon...

His mind was empty, carved out by whatever had been in the hookah, and words bounced slowly around inside it.

The dragon...

Hidden power...

Kermits with boobs...

"I'm going to go shower," he said mechanically. "Good night."

"Good night," came muffled from the prone Jonah.

4 THE WORM

Tony had already showered once before that day, knowing that his dear cousin would have simply walked away from him if he'd shown up with dirt under his fingernails, and generally for Tony one shower a day was enough. He wasn't one of those dudes who overdid it with the hand sanitizer and the flossing after every snack. He happily ate his lunch with dirty hands

But today, Tony jumped in the shower for the second time, now with the mental image of naked-and-bound Ezra Fontaine plastered to his eyelids, and greedily reacquainted himself with several old friends:

The shower wall, five inches of gently curving silicone with a suction cup base, and his prostate.

When it came time to 'dance,' Tony was a born top. He topped because it would have been *criminal* not to use the eight-and-a-quarter inches God had given him.

But in his solo time, he enjoyed slapping his wet cheeks against the shower walls as much as anyone.

He uncapped his shower lube, fingerbanged himself slick, and got to it.

Wedging the rounded head of the toy inside, chanting, unaware, under his breath, thinking of Fontaine, "Take it, bitch. Fucking take it."

Thinking of Fontaine bound in nothing but those little black shorts, thighs splayed.

Imagining that *under* the shorts, someone (which would have to be his cousin, but Tony cleanly repressed that detail) had plugged his ass with big, deep, vibrating beads.

Tony had beads.

He rode his shower toy hands free — face flushed, cock bouncing hard and awkward about his thighs — until the sizzling urge to shoot began to threaten, tightening in his balls, and then he went for his beads.

Not bothering to dress, still dripping wet from the shower, Tony walked down the plate glass of the short hall to his equally full-wall-glass windowed room, long dick bouncing with every stride.

One of the major perks of couch surfing in *this* family was the guaranteed privacy of its high rises.

Anyone opposite his window would have gotten a show, but there was simply no one to look in.

He was above the city, above the hoi polloi... above the *clouds*, he thought, in a very drunk-and-stoned way. He stood for a second, naked and hard, before the glass.

Just like the dragon.

He flipped a switch, and his dark room turned deep blue.

Mood lighting.

He threw himself onto the enormous bed, army-crawled over the swathes of luxurious sheets, comforter, pillows, their whites turned pale blue, to the bedside table where he yanked open a drawer.

He drew out his bedside lube. His bedside plug of anal beads.

He slid them up his ass, one by one, pausing after each to relish the sensation.

On the wall across from his bed, his reflection bounced back at him. Naked, blue, shredded, hair dark and shining wet.

He pressed in the final bead, letting the plug come to rest against his ass, and groaned.

He dragged a pillow down, between his legs, and humped it — but not too hard. Not too fast. Waiting, trying not to come, but relishing the smooth glide against his dick.

He took out his phone.

It wasn't the drugs, wasn't the alcohol bolstering him at that moment.

It wasn't the beads, the throbbing in his gut from dildo riding.

It wasn't even his own dick, hot and howling at him to knock this shit off and just come already.

No. Tony was seized by a different power altogether, something stronger and more potent, driving him to swipe through his phone, bring up the numbers, create the contact, and send a message to EZ fucking Ezra Fontaine.

He felt no fear.

He had nothing *to* fear.

He was a fucking sex god, his meat was huge, he was fucking *built* from gym and the job, and the silicone beads in his grinding, flexing ass as he pillow-humped were sending hot, stupid messages to his already hot, stupid, drunk, horny brain.

He was *the dragon*.

And the dragon texted:

> Hello, you lowly worm.

The dragon floated in the neon dark blue of the room. Glistening, hot, frotting his big dick on the silk pillow and thinking about round, muscle-thick ass, shiny-silver Fontaine getting down on his knees in his bespoke trousers, on the dirty concrete of the back garage.

He continued:

> I am going to own your ass.

He imagined parting Fontaine's lips with one finger, as if unzipping them.

> I'm going to make you suck me so deep you'll have a second Adam's apple.

He flashed back to Fontaine's sneer, the drumming of fingers on the countertop while someone searched for his keys. The expression on his face. The impatience. The look of 'I'm too important for this.'

'*I know all about you,*' the dragon continued. Reliving the man. The moment. The *picture*. He mashed together words with an almost manic zeal.

> You bad attitude sloppy mess spoiled sub whore.

He resisted actively jerking it, knowing he wouldn't last long, bobbing and bumping against the beads instead. Tempted to change the angle of his hips, he imagined — instead of frotting with his dick — grinding his ass down, against the pillow, fucking himself better.

He moved, typed, drunkenly. Seeing the echo of tarot in his mind's eye, the yellow slits of eyes glowering out of the shadows. *He* had those eyes. *He* was the 'master of all things.' The natural world was *his* dominion.

> I'll remind you what that body is for.

Text sent.

Text... read?

He stared at his phone.

Read 1:31 AM.

Tony would have felt reality crash around him, would have freaked and thrown the phone across the room.

But he wasn't Tony anymore.

He was *the dragon.*

And the dragon gleefully accelerated.

> You're better off without a husband, and you know why. It's because you're not husband material. Not boyfriend material. What you need is a MASTER.

Read 1:32 AM.

He thrust himself harder at the pillow, gnawing his lip, pumping relentlessly. A kind of sadistic, animal glee had seized him.

> You don't need a bed, you need a kennel.

> You don't need a tie, you need a collar.

> You need someone to tie you down and rough you up from behind until you remember:

Read 1:33 AM.

> Your role is to SERVE.

He was sweating. Trembling. Orgasm lurked everywhere in his body but his dick, making his toes and his earlobes scream, and he felt aware of every vein in his body standing out. He had never looked so cut. So hard. His cock was like the purple-black of the dragon from the tarot deck, everything in the room dark and blue or brilliant, tinted white.

Read 1:33 AM.

The idea of Fontaine reading the texts was too much. Finally, too much.

Tony switched to video.

Dropping back, splayed against the pillows, he gripped himself, he gripped the phone, and he recorded.

Dick fully in frame, throbbing against a backdrop of spread, muscled thighs and blue-lit white sheets. Long. Thick. Threatening.

His fingers wrapping around it.

He let himself moan.

He pumped with his hand, with his hips.

His eyes rolled back as he finally blasted off.

Later, Tony would watch the video and whistle appreciatively. It was a great shot! All his best features on display. Dick looking *spectacular*. Going off like uncorked champagne, his hand helping it along, pumping out cum that went from a sudden gush to fat dribbles.

As he came and his pelvic muscles all clenched, they closed like a fist around the anal beads.

His thighs jerked and went rigid again, quaking, and just as soon as the first wave had ended, the second seized him. His hand had barely slackened before it leapt into frenzied motion again.

He wouldn't think until later about his wrist tattoo, which was cleanly in frame.

A little cartoon unicorn sitting innocently on top of bulging veins and tendons.

He finished.

He sent the video.

And he flopped, feeling the warm rush of endorphins through every inch of his body, throbbing gently still around the fat beads.

He laughed drunkenly at the ceiling.

When his phone buzzed, his brain didn't immediately register that it *was* his phone, and he lay there wondering faintly what the noise was. Bzz. *Pause.* Bzz. *Pause.*

It was on the fourth pause that Tony sat bolt upright and grabbed his phone again.

He couldn't have explained why he answered, or what the hell he expected. What he *should* have expected were threats of violence and a promise that the police were tracing this call.

But he answered.

And what he *got* was the sound of a man beating off with all his might.

Hoarse, ragged panting.

A desperate gasp of, "Call me a worm again."

"Worm," supplied Tony helpfully.

Ezra Fontaine came with a shameless, full-throated moan.

5 EGGTOOTH

Tony dreamed the life cycle of a dragon.

There was the egg, of course — the result of two chomping, snarling, twining, glittering monsters, serpents with wings and claws and jeweled scales. One was iridescent purple-black, like the tarot card, the other white touched with gold. They fought a battle that became a dance. And at the end of it was a clutch of eggs.

Dull, stony gray colored eggs.

They blended in with the stone of the rock crags, two dozen of them in all. *His* stood out no more than the rest. There was no sign that this egg bore the developing, beating heart of an emperor inside of it.

Until hatching time.

His shell was the first to crack, his hard eggtooth the first to break through the barrier into life, and his yellow eyes the first to squint against the dancing mountain auroras.

The black mother and white father had remained close enough to surveil the clutch from a distance. As the eggs began to hatch, they went on the hunt, and soon returned with clumps of bloody flesh and viscera, showering drops of gore on their then-shrieking egg-damp offspring.

Dragon young grew rapidly. The very weakest never made it out of their eggs, and the weakest after that were soon shoved gleefully from the nest by their stronger brothers and sisters. Feeding time was always a tournament; the largest and most aggressive grew larger and more aggressive, as they shouldered aside their siblings to get the best of the carnage.

Eventually, the night mother and sun father brought live food.

The weakest did not survive long, once the strongest of the clutch had developed a taste for thrashing prey.

It took only days after that before the first of them — Tony was first out of all, obviously — began stretching and flapping their wings, screeching in the cracked, garbled voices of infancy still. By the time they were able to clamber up to the rim of the nest, to look out over the vast valleys and rocky mountain spires, their voices had strengthened. They shrieked like eagles. They snarled like wolves.

The time came.

Mother and father watched from nearby crags, as still and silent as statues, while their largest son crawled up to the apex of the nest.

Tony wobbled at the edge of the nest, got his balance, and spread his wings.

The sleek black dragonlet, his undersides spotty with white scintillations to mimic the night sky, dropped off the edge and fell away into gliding twilight.

The years that followed were bloody ones.

A juvenile dragon was a mindless, hungry thing, and Tony was no exception. He was concerned only with stuffing his face and falling asleep on a warm rock somewhere. Many draconic young fell prey to other creatures — rocs, manticores, men and their snares — but the best of them grew with astonishing speed, and Tony was the *best* of the best! No roc, manticore, or man *dared* accost the young dragon who ballooned quickly to the size of a horse, then a buffalo, then a rhinoceros.

Maturity came with a plume of color.

One morning, after a particularly *grueling* shed — Tony had been forced to grovel about in the mud, softening the itchy old skin and then grinding it away on rocks, working at it for hours — the dragon entered deep water as a dark, patchy juvenile... and emerged resplendent.

The dark underside remained, but on top, he had come into his true colors.

From the thorny tip of his snout to the crest of horns ringing his head, following the spines of his neck and blanketing his shoulders, spilling over his back and the tops of his wings, all the way down his tail to the vicious prong at the end, he was a brilliant red.

Not the red of blood and viscera, but that of deeply flushing roses.

And with color came *intellect*.

Soon, the dragon Tony overflew the valley and lit on a mountain cliff to look down at the world of man.

Industry! Mining, farming. The building of roads, houses, stone walls. Churning water mills, wagons pulled by teams of horses, and at the end of it all, a great city.

And at the peak of the great city was a great palace.

Tony thought to himself that he was a *great* dragon.

Princely.

Kingly, perhaps?

His toothy maw stretched into a grotesque grin, lipless, tongue flickering bloodred behind the cage of fangs.

And Tony the human awoke with a "HWAGH," as his alarm went off, and crashed sideways out of bed.

He lay for a moment on the floor. He said "Hwagh," again, this time in a groan, and touched a budding goose-egg on his forehead where he had knocked it on the bedside table.

He rolled over onto his back to gaze at the high ceiling.

The first thing he remembered was not the party, or the dirty text messages, or Fontaine's moan coming through the receiver.

It was the *dragon*.

The dream itself was floating away as quickly as dreams often did, the taste of viscera and the sensation of flying both lost to him in a matter of blinked moments, but the final image remained.

And more powerful than the final image — perched on a high cliff, leering down at the conquerable kingdom below — was the *feeling!*

The glorious confidence of the dragon.

'The master of all things.'

Though his body ached from the night's abuse and the morning's rude awakening, Tony's mind bubbled over with a gloating sense of conviction.

It was going to be a good day.

"SPIDER MONKEY," boomed Milo's voice for the third time that morning, as Tony almost dropped a car hood on his head. He straightened up, fuming, slightly sunburned face redder with anger.

"My b," said Tony. "My b my b. You okay?" He threw his greasy palms up in apology and nearly brained Milo with a wrench. "Uhhh. My b."

Milo — grizzled, ex military, and almost as tall as Tony, which was saying something — pierced the apprentice mechanic with a frosty gaze that would have terrified anyone less affable.

"Are you trying to kill me, or do *you* want to die today?" he demanded.

"All right all right," came a voice, no louder than theirs, but carrying a ring of pursed-lips authority.

Mayhew emerged from his office with one hand on his hip, and it seemed like it would have been both hands on hips if he hadn't needed one to hold his coffee. He looked as irritated as he did hungover.

"What's wrong with you?" he demanded of Tony. "All thumbs, all morning. Party too hard last night?"

Tony pouched his lips in thought, the thought being '*Well, yeah,*' but the *partying* was not the problem.

The problem was his constant mental replaying of the texts, the image of Ezra Fontaine bound with rope, the sound of the older man's moans, and all the burning, boiling, distracting fantasies and questions which came with alllll of the above.

Tony's brain, not used to carrying more than one tune at a time, was too crammed with *stuff* to be capable of *work*.

"Sorry, boss," he said. He carefully — apologetically, even — put down the wrench and put out his hands in apology. "I, uh. I. Uhhh…"

No excuse was coming to mind.

Milo and the rest of the guys — Skippy, Skillets, Sasha, Turner, Ross — waited for one, eyebrows raised, looking variably amused and skeptical and annoyed.

But Mayhew didn't wait for an excuse.

"Come back here," he ordered, jabbing a thumb over his shoulder at the office door. "I wanta minute."

He turned on his heel, went back in, and Tony obediently trotted after.

This wasn't the prim, tidy customer-facing office up front, but the back office which contained all the fuckery and whatsits necessary for smoothly running a shop like this. Dusty file cabinets. Big-ass oak desk, size of a small boat. A wallful of calendars — Playboy bunnies, sexy fireman — printer and cobwebby-dead fax machine. Most importantly, the one way glass. Two sides of it. One view of his mechanics. Another of the front desk. Ideal.

Mayhew sat down in his special, ergonomic wheely-chair behind the desk and beckoned for Tony to sit in the creaky little steel one in front.

"Whatsamatter, kid?" demanded Mayhew. "You've been stepping it up lately; I was *this* close to proud." He held his thumb and forefinger together, almost touching. "You know, I wasn't gonna hire you, when you first walked in and I saw that stupid haircut. But you proved me wrong."

Tony didn't know what to say to that. He just said "Huh," in a voice he hoped sounded thoughtful, or thankful, or whatever Mayhew wanted from him.

"Don't fuck it up now." Mayhew wagged a finger at him. He would have been very mommish if he had not been sixty-something and covered in sun-faded biker ink.

"I won't," said Tony, with an earnest double thumbs up and a winning smile.

Neither the thumbs up or the winning smile seemed to make Mayhew happy. The man pursed his lips, gave a dissatisfied grunt, and, pulling out his wallet, grubbed around until he found a twenty.

"Here," he said, shoving it over at Tony. "Go take an early lunch, and make it a long one. Get your head on straight. Remember; you're staying late to do handover with Mr. Fontaine."

Tony's freely galloping mind made the SCREEEE of stomped on brakes.

It must have shown in his face; Mayhew stood up and gave him a commiserating slap on the back.

"I know the guy's an ass," he said. "Just play it lowkey and give him the keys, no problem. You'll live, kid."

Mayhew hitched at his overalls, gave Tony another back-slap, and went back out the door to go yell at Skippy about something.

Tony sat on the curb under trees and blue sky, in a secluded corner of the parking lot, with an uneaten sandwich in one hand and phone in the other.

He scrolled through last night's texts with a sense of impending doom that only somewhat dampened his boner.

> You need someone to tie you down and rough you up from behind until you remember:
>
> Your role is to SERVE.

The video.

He had really sent those texts, huh? He had *really* sent that video, huh?

They had spoken on the phone only briefly, just long enough for Tony to call Fontaine a worm and make him come, and Tony *doubted* that the single word 'worm' would be enough for Fontaine to recognize him when he came to grab those keys.

But then… didn't Tony kind of *want* him to?

Wasn't that the goal? To eventually say that shit in person? To *do* something in person… *to* that person?

This shit hadn't come up in his conversation with cousin Zachary.

And that was when the lightbulb flicked on in Tony's head.

Goff answered his call two rings in.

"Just so you know," Goff opened. "I *only* picked up because it was a convenient way to ditch a conversation with a different pain in the ass cousin. What do you want that couldn't wait until after business hours?" His tone suddenly changed, somewhere between hopeful and mean-glee. "You didn't get fired, did you?"

"I fucked up," said Tony. He put his palm to his forehead, closed his eyes, and groaned his despair into the receiver.

"I'm shocked," said Goff. "What happened?"

Tony spilled it all.

Stealing Fontaine's number. Drinking. Smoking. The dragon card. The texts. The video.

The phone call.

He concluded his story with another anguished groan, a fresh wave of dread sweeping over him, and rubbed his palm aggressively against his forehead.

"I'm staying late to hand over his keys," he said. "What do I do?"

Silence from Goff.

Tony, who had expected either laughter or a glib *'don't care, good luck,'* glanced at the phone to check they were still connected.

"Actually," said his cousin after a moment, sounding as if he were loath to admit this. "You might not be in such a bad position."

"Huh?" Tony frowned, brow crinkling. "What do you mean?"

"I mean," said Goff, in a voice that said he was still thinking, "that you haven't *really* fucked it up yet, have you?"

"I haven't?"

"You've never spoken to him *in person*, correct?"

"Yeah."

"So all you did was send him a series of nasty messages and a cumshot, and you had him panting in your ear begging to be called a worm, correct?"

"Umm." Tony recollected. "Yeah?"

"So," Goff went on slowly, with an insulting kind of patience, like he was explaining something to a toddler. "He doesn't know you're a neanderthal... yet. He thinks you're Mr. Big Dick come out of nowhere to fulfill his fantasies."

"*Does* he?" Tony's mouth formed a round O of surprise; that possibility hadn't occurred to him *at all*.

"I think..." Goff paused, mulled. "I think that if you keep your trap shut ninety-nine percent of the time, you *might* be able to get away with it. You don't *look* stupid. And you look much older than you are. He might mistake you for a real life Mr. Big Dick."

Tony let the half-insult, half-compliment bounce off of him, focusing on strategy.

"But if I 'keep my trap shut' ninety-nine percent of the time, how am I supposed to... you know, get anywhere? *Do* anything?"

"This is 'EZ' Ezra, remember?" drawled Goff. "Don't overthink it. Let him do the talking. *You* do the grabbing."

Tony sat there for a moment, letting his overthinking dissolve into a blank, white haze of '*huh.*' Trying to decide if any of this made sense.

Goff clicked his tongue thoughtfully. "Let's see..."

He trailed off, and again Tony checked his phone to make sure he hadn't been hung up on.

"I think we can test this theory," said Goff then, sounding entertained, and not in a comforting way. In a nearly sadistic-*gleeful* way. He had gone into planning mode. "All right, listen. This is what you're going to do."

Tony listened.

He sat there for a while, listening, his completely forgotten sandwich going stale in his hand. When his cousin finished and finally *did* hang up on him, Tony sat there still for a minute with the phone to his ear, before slowly lowering it back to his lap.

He looked out across the parking lot.

For a minute he was rational, thinking, *'Of course not. This is crazy. This whole thing is crazy.'*

And then his mind reset itself.

It *sneered* at his rationality. His restraint.

Why should he restrain himself from doing what he wanted? *Taking* what he wanted?

He was *the dragon*.

And the dragon swiped through his phone, finding the short chain of filthy texts from the night before.

He sent one more.

A *command*.

6 EMPLOYEE PARKING ONLY

It didn't take Ezra Fontaine long to comply.

The picture came from indoors; Tony saw a sliver of dark wooden wall, a glimpse of rustic-pretentious hanging lamp. Just enough to make a little question mark ping in Tony's mind, to make him wonder where Fontaine was if not in some high rise office.

The question mark was booted aside immediately, as he zeroed in on the focus of the picture.

Fontaine was in a suit. The photo framed him from the lower jaw to above mid-torso — not much. Tony saw the tie, blue, pulled aside. The shirt buttons undone — not all of them. Just a few.

Just enough for Fontaine to have exposed a single nipple, glimpsed through the sliver of parted fabric.

Tony's breath caught.

His mouth filled with the taste of metal.

Fontaine's nipple was pierced through with a golden barbell, each end topped with a tiny ruby.

In all of Tony's fantasies about the stone cold fox, *piercings* had never played a role. Why would they have? One look at Ezra Fontaine's stiff presentation — the suits, the diamond timepieces, the unsmiling sharp edge of him — was enough to dismiss the idea that *this* man ever got holes punched in his body for vanity.

And yet the tiny rubies gleamed.

For vanity...

The idea played about in Tony's head, taking different shapes.

Was it for vanity?

If not, then... what?

Tony imagined fingertips rolling over that barbell, clasping the nipple as it hardened. Pinching. Grinding together sensitive skin and metal.

Imagined Fontaine's moaning — just as he had heard it over the phone.

Tony knew immediately that continuing this text chain out in broad daylight would be an impossibility.

...But he also couldn't just waltz back into the shop, returned early from his 'long lunch' and excuse himself to the bathroom for however long this took.

Fortunately, he had a third option.

His car sat out back, in the cluttered alley marked with 'EMPLOYEE PARKING ONLY' which none of the regular employees used because of the pigeons that tended to shit everywhere. Tony's adorable beater — a tiny white Kimura Renegade that looked like a clown car with giant Tony driving it, knees drawn up and elbows hanging out — was crappy enough that extra crap felt inconsequential.

The door whined in rusty protest as he opened it, hopped in, shut it. The tiny little car rocked with the weight of his climbing in. He adjusted his seat back and got cozy.

Tony had just gotten settled and unzipped when the next picture came.

This shot was slightly more... avant-garde.

Again Tony saw the gap between opened buttons, but this time one button had been done back up. The gap was smaller, and spread open with two fingers. Creating a careful window in order to catch both nipples in one shot.

They were *both* pierced.

The words 'choking hazards' leapt to Tony's drooling-hungry mind.

More erotic than the piercings, however, was the photo's composition. Strangely angled. Taken up close, only barely managing to make the shot. Buttons done back up.

And Tony realized.

Fontaine was *sneaking* the pictures.

He was either not alone, or he was somewhere in public.

Or both.

Tony barely had to tug down his waistband to free his cock; it sprang out almost violently, rebound-bobbing in its eagerness.

He spat in his hand and gave his old friend a good, long stroke of greeting.

He texted:

> Rub those nips for your Master, worm.

It took several minutes for the next picture, during which Tony gripped the base of his dick and waited patiently, all his will compressed to a diamond-hard focus.

Fontaine's response was not a picture.

It was a video.

The clip was only a few seconds long. Tony saw the white shirtfront, buttons lined up evenly as *if* done up... but they were not. Fontaine's long, perfectly manicured fingers abruptly parted them, baring a single nipple and its exotic glint of gold and ruby.

The nipple was completely hard. Rigid.

Fontaine's thumb planted over it and rubbed, back and forth, a movement almost like trying to ease some discomfort.

But it kept rubbing. Firmer. Then more so. *Rough*, now. *Pushing* the barbell back and forth, *punishing* the tender skin underneath.

And abruptly it stopped, pulled shut the shirt fabric again, and the video cut off.

Tony's hard-on *raged*.

What kind of fucking *torment!*

But he had glimpsed more of the background in the short clip, and as he replayed it, he realized Fontaine was in some kind of shop.

A tailor shop, he thought. He saw bolts of cloth, a wall of ties, a set of pull-out drawers displaying pocket squares. It looked upscale. It *had* to be upscale.

A fresh thrill went through Tony — a smug one.

You only had to catch one glimpse of Fontaine to know the man valued his wardrobe. He never had so much as a cufflink out of place. Tony expected he went to one of those exorbitant spots Goff frequented, the kind Tony's mother had trapped him in a few times before. He would have bet money that Fontaine blocked off a whole *day* for this. The fitting. The alterations. Head to toe, shoes and socks to a new set of ties and hell, throw in another hundred dollar haircut.

And yet Fontaine had allowed Tony and his big, fat, eight-and-a-quarter inch dick to interrupt.

Tony smiled.

He replayed the video. He replayed it a few times.

He watched the older man thumb *desperately* at his nipple, working it like someone might work their cock, with a rough and hungry lack of rhythm.

Tony realized he was almost drooling, literally, and loudly sucked back and swallowed his own spit.

He sent another message.

> Give your Master a real show.

The delay in response didn't bother him.

It was *delicious*.

And the result was worth it.

Another clip, this one slightly longer, and no longer the shaky-camera self-filming style.

Fontaine had propped his phone up on something. He stood there, in some slightly narrower, dimmer space — A back room, maybe? A little corridor between chambers? — with a rack of muted pastel shirts behind him. The camera caught him from chin-height to *just* below the belt.

Just enough to see the shadow of a thick bulge. A 'slipped the boxer elastic down to show you this' bulge.

His tie was loosened and pushed aside, haphazard. His shirt open halfway, a gaping V that ran from throat to just above his navel.

Both piercings glinted in the low light. Twin soft gleamings that disappeared, reappeared, and disappeared again as Fontaine caressed himself.

Taking big, squeezing handfuls of his own pecs. Taking long, *firm* pulls on his nipples. Pinching them. Drawing them out. *Twisting* them.

Tony leaned in as if his nose wasn't already an inch from the screen, turning up the brightness, trying to decide if he was imagining or not that Fontaine was actually *digging his nails in.*

'Give your Master a real show,' he had said.

And Fontaine did just that.

Stepped forward, leaned in, pecs coming close into focus. They dominated the screen, *tormenting* Tony by not being in his mouth that very second.

A slight pause.

Then a spitting sound. Just offscreen.

Fontaine's fingers came back into view... glistening with saliva.

He delicately painted it onto his nipples. Making them glisten, wet. Glossy. Shining.

The delicacy of the gesture, compared to the extreme roughness before, nearly sent Tony over the edge.

The clip ended, and Tony fumed.

He was equal parts tormented and ecstatic. He *wanted*. He wanted more than he had ever wanted in his life. And the thing he wanted was *right there*... and also completely out of reach.

Stunted desire brought on a rare, strange flare of the sadistic.

He sent:

> Nasty slut whore.

And,

> So eager to please a big dick stranger.

And,

> Sloppy disgusting worm.

And then, a plume of inspiration:

> Why don't you show your Master what a lowly worm you really are?

This time the delay was longer.

A different Tony might have assumed he'd lost Fontaine's interest, sheepishly jerked off and moved on.

But this Tony was something different.

Something with sharp teeth, and cold blood to balance out all that hot lust.

The Dragon waited.

And Fontaine obeyed his command. *Succumbed* to it.

Pictures this time.

Tony thumbed slowly through them.

Fontaine had found a changing room. Tony saw a full length dressing mirror, antiquelike. A tufted wingback chair, its leather tinted red. The room was dark, intimate, an old style. Overhead was a warm and gold-glowing chandelier, casting soft light.

Behind it all, a red curtain.

If Tony had been more of an aesthete, he might have admired how Fontaine had used the space.

Fontaine rested one hand on the back of the chair for balance, holding his phone in the other, body arced carefully around to capture the shot of himself in the full length mirror.

Tony couldn't see much detail; the light was too soft. But he could see that Fontaine's shirt was fully unbuttoned, hanging open. Could see that his tie was discarded, draped over the arm of the chair. Couldn't quite see the face of the man, or the expression — just the dark outline of his profile — but *could* see the strong square of his jaw. Hot. Masculine.

Fontaine had dropped trou to about midthigh.

He did not *bend over* in a truly crass, slutty way. Did not obviously arch his back or thrust out his ass.

He bent only a little.

Arched his back *just* a little.

And offered his ass to the mirror — to the camera, to Tony's starved eyes — *just* enough so that the soft, warm light of the chandelier could trickle between his legs and catch sharply on the bright, metallic something that glinted there.

Tony noisily swallowed his spit again.

He thumbed through the pictures to see Fontaine reaching between his legs. Pushing his hard cock back. Into view, into the light of the overhead bulbs.

It was a big, *thick* dick, just as Tony had glimpsed through his pant leg on that one fateful day.

Exactly the kind Tony loved to watch bounce around as he fucked the helplessly orgasming owner.

Exactly the kind he loved to *frot on,* to grab and grind alongside his own, *bigger* dick, humiliating the owner. Making the other man look. Making other man — the preferably much *older* man — feel how *small* he was by comparison.

And the kind he loved to *grab,* to playfully twist, to tug and pull and mock as he was stuffing the owner's ass with something *much* bigger.

But with one key difference.

It had a piercing.

A large, heavy looking ring fixed through the head.

Tony was in flames. Part of it was almost *anger.* How dare Fontaine be so *fine,* so high and mighty and above everyone else in the world, and yet so droolingly fuckable. Untouchable. Pantingly desirable.

He demanded:

> Crawl on the ground for your Master.
>
> Crawl like the worm you are.

He wanted, *needed* to see Fontaine on the ground. On his knees. Debased. Brought *down.*

He *craved* it.

Fontaine apparently craved the same thing.

Now video came again.

At an awkward angle of a propped-up phone, Tony saw the man on all fours in front of the mirror, bent down, almost prone.

Fontaine was facing away from the mirror.

This time with hips raised, back well-arched, and thighs spread, he presented himself fully to the mirror. Metal plug shining between his legs. Face pressed almost to the floor. Looking back at the camera, looking to make sure it caught all of him, that his *Master* could see all of him.

Fontaine's hand moved slowly between his legs, rubbing his dangling cock.

No... not *rubbing*.

Displaying.

Offering.

The ring in the head gleaming, catching and casting off light.

Watching vapidly, Tony suddenly noticed the rise and fall of Fontaine's chest, and it occurred to him to check for sound. Hoping to catch the man panting, he unmuted.

Tony caught more than panting.

There was, in the background, the sound of muffled voices.

They were muffled *only* by the red curtains.

Fontaine was doing this only feet away from other human beings, other people, potential witnesses.

Tony realized in that moment his true power.

He realized, too, the true *depth* of Fontaine's submission, the desperate subservience the man offered in the mirror. In his reflection. In this video. This was something Fontaine had been craving for a *long* time. Tony sensed it, but could only guess how long.

And Tony, out of the generosity of his heart, sent back an offering of his own:

A picture of his big, *FAT* dick next to his thick, muscular forearm. Close up with veins and all.

Tony sent the picture.

And a little extra.

> This is what you serve, Worm.
>
> This is your Lord and Master.

The following video of Fontaine — visibly trembling, gripping his cock like it might go off like a bomb — blurred as the man reached for his phone, pulled it into shadow around his face. He whispered:

"Yes."

There, only feet from who knows how many people, Ezra Fontaine whispered a desperate, ecstatic:

"Yes, Master."

And Fontaine was even such an old pro at the game, he even threw in a, "Thank you, Master."

Tony replayed the ragged whispers right against his ear.

He held tight to his dick. *Real* tight.

Not yet, not yet.

A challenge:

> How would you please your Master? What can YOU do in service for your Lord?

Nothing but darkness in Fontaine's video response, maybe some faint movement, and a hoarse but fervent whispering.

"Suck you all the way down my throat, deep enough to lick your balls at the same time."

That did it.

Tony spasmed, cock rebelling in his hand, cum pumping out of him before he could even grab a discarded takeout napkin to catch it. He didn't care. He flogged himself, gasping, groaning, pumping out each burst of ecstasy.

He didn't have to ask Fontaine to send him a cumshot.

The final video was something of a miracle; Tony had no idea how the hell the light and phone angle managed to catch *just* the right moment, the right part of Fontaine's body. There was no way he could have done it on purpose.

It shot between Fontaine's legs, showed the bobbing of his cock, the hand wrapped around it, the heavy ring dancing in the air.

The sudden seizure of muscles, and the spouting, shooting. Eyes rolling.

Fontaine managed to bite back any real noise. Instead Tony heard his breath rattling, the muffled panting against skin, the click of teeth trying to bite back bliss.

The sound of *victory*.

7 SHARPIE

Tony was no more useful after jacking it than he had been before.

However, his coworkers seemed to have resigned themselves to doing Tony's tasks as well as their own, keeping him far away from anything dangerous or important and leaving him to float in a haze of reliving Fontaine's *everything*.

Little ruby-tipped, golden barbells with the nipples hard underneath them.

The firm, sculpted muscle of those thighs, that ass.

His *voice*.

The more Tony thought about it, the more it drove him bananas.

There was a horny, fucked up, addictive paradox there. Even in those groveling, subservient moments, Fontaine had somehow still sounded like himself. Debased, but *distinguished*. Silvery. Slutty. Lordly. Dethroned. All of it.

It was inexplicable. Bananas.

Standing at his station, leaning on a car, barely pretending to work, Tony's eyes glazed over and he was *consumed* by it. It. The paradox. The man.

How could Ezra Fontaine be on the floor of a tailor shop, ass up, recording himself for a stranger he knew only as a big dick and dirty texter, nipples pierced, *dick* pierced, ass plugged, and still have that... that...

...that air of frost.

Not *cold*, exactly. Not 'frost' as in icy, but in some way... crisp. Cool. Only a few degrees separated from disdainful, from arrogant, but they were *key* degrees.

Still himself.

"TONY!" boomed a voice.

Yikes. Not 'Spider Monkey,' but 'Tony.'

He quickly looked up, put on his most winningest smile, said, "Yes?"

Sasha and Perry stood there glowering, Perry with a big, fresh red mark on his forehead. Tony opened his mouth to ask what happened, and then it occurred to him that whatever happened, probably happened because he wasn't paying attention.

They didn't even bother to yell at him, nothing more than his name.

"Kid's got his head in the clouds," said Perry instead, turning away in disgust.

Head in the clouds. That was a generously clean way of putting it.

Sasha shook his head. "Why don't you go sort paperclips in the office, Tony?"

"You got it," said Tony instantly, putting three fingers to his forehead in a Boy Scout salute.

Of course, he spent his time in the office reviewing and re-reviewing his texts.

He couldn't help but admire his own work. *Great* cumshot. *Great* dick pic. Even his *texts* were solid, somehow managing to sell the farce that Tony was more than a nineteen-year-old horndog blessed with a bigger dick than he deserved.

But then again. Maybe he *was* more than a nineteen-year-old horndog with a bigger dick than he deserved.

After all, no one had dictated these texts for him. They had come from *somewhere* in his brain. Some sneaky, hidden corner, where another fragment of mind lurked. A cleverer, sharper fragment which normally slumped in a bean bag chair, smoking a bong, but reared its head eagerly when a silver fox with body mods appeared.

The dragon.

He could feel it thrilling in his bones as he re-regarded his growing collection... his bones, and other places.

But Tony wasn't an *animal*.

He waited for everyone else to clock out and shove off before he whipped his dick out.

"You know you're staying late, right?" Milo reminded him, shoving his head in the door and looking at Tony suspiciously as if knowing *exactly* what his apprentice was going to do. Milo had a rain slicker slung over his shoulder, toolbox in hand, eyes narrowed.

"Yep." Tony, sitting back in Mayhew's chair, feet up on the desk, gave a double thumbs up. "I'm gonna sort all the paperclips."

"Uh huh." Milo squinted at him for another moment, distrusting, then seemed to decide that whatever Tony was up to, it wasn't worth his attention. "Remember to lock up."

"Got it," said Tony, still holding up both thumbs.

Milo wordlessly let the door swing shut.

He strode off, the last mechanic in the shop, and out the side door he went.

Tony whipped it out.

He didn't *use* to be that guy; he had even given himself an ultimatum when he started working in the shop and, on his first day, found it populated mostly by DILFs. Ex military welders. Wealthy older car enthusiasts flashing their keys and cash around. Grumpy veterans of the industry, who could knock out an engine change in four hours flat while not missing a beat in their rant about the economy.

DILFs, DILFs, DILFs.

Tony's natural hunting ground.

But he had controlled himself, refused to allow so much as an eyelash bat or lower lip bite, or a 'Let me help you with that, my fellow coworker' bicep squeeze.

And he had meticulously stuck to his un-horny role until Fontaine.

Who was so foxy, so DILFy, so hot, and apparently *so* down for it, that Tony was unmanned.

The dragon had him by the balls and wasn't about to let go.

So Tony, 'working' late, happily spanked one out in the boss's office. His second of the day.

He jizzed carefully in a kleenex, put it in the trash, took the trash out, and thoroughly washed his hands.

He wasn't an *animal*.

And it was in that post-spank warm mental fuzz, content in the knowledge that he was a good person, that Tony heard a strange ringing noise.

He frowned.

He looked around the office, stuck one finger in his ear and wiggled it. He hadn't come *that* hard, had he?

Ring ring.

And then it struck him, brilliant as a diamond bullet, right to the forehead. Memory.

'I can pick it up between six and eight-thirty tomorrow. Will there be someone here to handle keys?'

'Tony will be here. He'll take care of you.'

Tony's eyes shot to the clock.

7:01.

Oh no.

Ezra Fontaine didn't even look up when Tony opened the front door.

He simply walked briskly inside, his focus on something coming through his Bluetooth earpiece, a passing cloud of droolworthy cologne.

Piercing eyes. They had not been visible in either the pictures or videos, and Tony had almost forgotten about their sea-glass razor edge.

"Kimura Cloud," was all Fontaine said, his attention still on whoever was speaking. He didn't say it *to* Tony; he simply floated the name of his car into the garage air and waited for it to magically appear.

It wasn't *insulting*, exactly. It was just the manner of a man of Fontaine's caliber. He *expected* good, prompt service wherever he went, whenever he needed it. Why?

Because he was used to getting it.

Tony nearly reeled with the desire to grab Fontaine by the hair and pound the attitude out of him, on all fours right there on the lobby floor.

Then Fontaine *did* look at him, when the garage Igor didn't instantly scramble to do his bidding, a light frown creasing his forehead.

For an instant their eyes met.

And that was when Tony realized that mercilessly dominating a man over text message was *not* the same thing as doing it in person.

In fact, he could hardly imagine *anyone* dominating this man.

Ezra Fontaine stood there like a fine-as-fuck statue, spine straight, posture immaculate, suit pristinely cresting over his perfectly built muscles, but he was like a statue carved *not* out of marble but of iron fucking girders.

Tony tried to revisualize the picture Zachary Goff had shown him. Tried to make the man in front of him resemble that picture. The pictures and *videos* currently on his *own* fucking phone!

He couldn't do it.

The dragon might have summited Mt. Fontaine with ease, but Tony the greasemonkey simply mumbled something about "—go pull it around front—" and slunk off to fetch the man's Kimura.

With Fontaine behind him, Tony marveled at his own blinking-caveman blankness.

It wasn't cowardice. He wasn't *cowed* by the older man.

He just couldn't find it in him to do anything but revert to supporting cast. The default.

It was a lot of fucking pressure!

Tony found Fontaine's raspberry Kimura parked out back and moodily climbed in, grumbling to himself about "Oh, the dragon, huh?" and "Good fucking grief," and he pulled the car around front.

He saw Fontaine through the glass as he pulled up and parked, saw him seeming to be having an animated conversation with *somebody* about *something*. Tony got out, taking the keys with him, and stood under the overhang. He riffled the keys through his fingers and mulled his options.

What options?

He supposed — his heart heavy — that debased text messages were all he was going to get out of this scenario.

Fontaine finally noticed him.

Fontaine tapped his earpiece, ending the call, adjusted his jacket, and stepped outside.

His gray-green eyes skimmed his car, examining every inch. He must have decided he was satisfied with the work, because he didn't say anything, only held out his hand for the keys.

Tony handed them over.

Fontaine did not say thank you.

No thank you, no eye contact, no human acknowledgment, he just took the keys and he passed Tony a folded hundred.

Tony could have shrugged all of that off.

But then Fontaine's eyes drifted over his clothes for just a beat of a second.

Tony's clothes weren't *filthy*, and they weren't peasant brands, either, but they were worked-in. He probably had a spot of grime here or there. He worked in a fucking *garage*.

But in that sliver of a glance, Tony saw Fontaine notice every single spot or speck, saw him picturing them sitting in and driving *his* car, saw not disdain or anything truly ugly but just a kind of disapproval. Maybe a touch of resignation. A flash of 'I'll need to have it wiped down... but then, that's the cost of coming down here.'

And that was the start of it.

Something *petty*.

If Tony hadn't been born with money, if something in him hadn't chafed and said *'hey, fuck you, man, a hundred? You think I eat gruel and live in a cardboard box? You expect me to bow down and kiss your shoes?'* nothing would have happened.

"Actually, you need to come in back," said Tony, thumbing towards the doors, towards the locked and darkened offices. "Something to sign."

Fontaine frowned.

Now he finally looked *at* Tony, into his face.

"Sign what?"

Crisp, gratifying annoyance.

Tony gave his best *'I don't know man, I just work here'* mindless greasemonkey shrug, thumbs hooked in pockets, shoulders slumped with bored teenage apathy.

"Mayhew left it out," he said.

Fontaine was far too classy to roll his eyes or let his frown deepen to a scowl.

He simply said "Fine," in a clipped voice.

Tony led him back.

He honest to God didn't have any intentions beyond wasting Fontaine's time.

Back in Mayhew's office, he found a bullshit form in the file of bullshit forms. He presented it to Fontaine along with a pen he *knew* didn't work and sat down in his absent boss's chair, tossing a stress ball back and forth between his hands and waiting to see if Fontaine sat in the shitty little metal chair.

Fontaine glanced at it.

He did not sit down.

He skimmed the form, clearly identified it as bullshit, but said nothing. Of course not. He was *above* a customer service rant.

He began to sign. His brows pinched together.

"This pen doesn't work."

"Oh," said Tony, not even affecting surprise. Time for his master stroke.

He produced a Sharpie from his pocket and put it on the table. He slid it over.

Fontaine looked down at the grubby marker.

Tony saw, warring in him, the desire not to use the marker. Not to sign his signature *in marke*r. *Especially* not a marker pulled from the pockets of a dirty greasemonkey.

It was apparently too much for him to tolerate.

Fontaine opened his mouth, began to look up and say something. Tony, pleased as punch, waited for the complaint.

But Fontaine didn't say anything.

His eyes had frozen on something.

Following his gaze, glancing down, Tony's own gaze landed on the unicorn tattoo on his wrist.

The very prominent, *obvious* tattoo that would have been apparent in both dick pic and cumshot video.

Silence rang out between them like a gunshot.

In that silence Tony went completely still, stress ball stopped in one hand, no longer bouncing back and forth.

Fontaine stared at the tattoo for what felt like a full minute, expression frozen completely in the moment of realization.

And then his gaze slowly rose to Tony's.

And the dragon...

The dragon took wing.

That which had been waiting somewhere deep inside suddenly broke free, and Tony calmly put down the stress ball, reached down, and unzipped.

The *zzzzttt* was loud in the utterly still air of the office.

He stood and, businesslike, sagged his pants down and let Tony Jr. flop out like a distended, fat worm.

"You said you would suck me all the way down your throat, deep enough to lick my balls at the same time," he said calmly. "Go ahead."

He *sounded* calm.

He was *not*.

His exterior was a cold glaze on top of hot lava, a sheen like glass, and inside he *bubbled*. His body felt bizarrely light. He felt far away from himself and yet utterly *like* himself. He was coming alive. Coming awake.

His heart throbbed with hot, hot blood as Fontaine stared at him, still frozen, still shocked. Green-gray eyes wide.

Tony visualized Ezra Fontaine on his knees, mouth open, tongue out. He imagined his own eyes were balls of pure ice. He imagined he was eight feet tall with horns and a crown on his head, lounging on a throne made of skulls.

He put the full might of the dragon into his gaze. Lofty. Almost *sneering*. Entitled, awaiting.

And Fontaine *dropped his eyes*.

He took in the sight of Tony's seven inches — and that was seven inches *limp* — and his Adam's apple bobbed as he swallowed. His tongue wet his lips.

Nervous? Hungry? Anticipating?

All of the above.

And then Fontaine finally unfroze.

Unfroze and came forward, around the edge of the desk to his *Master*, and there he sank to his knees. It was a boneless, almost helpless sinking down. A man run through with a sword, fallen on the battlefield. Defeated.

His breath huffed on the head of Tony's cock.

Tony felt the hot breath, felt his balls go tight and his asshole clench.

Fontaine reached for it with one hand and Tony *growled* at him:

"Use your *mouth*. Put that hand away."

It was the commanding growl of the dragon.

If there had been any hesitation in Fontaine's response before, it faded now. He *knew* his Master, knew the rhythm and ritual of servility, and instantly he obeyed.

He put his hand away.

He leaned forward, rose up, and caught the head of Tony's cock between his lips.

And he began to suck him.

Tony was not surprised that Fontaine was fucking *incredible* at it.

Velvety. Wet. Snug. Hugging. *Tantalizing.*

Fontaine latched on and dragged the seal of his mouth back and forth over the tip, delivering long, firm, steady pulls of his lips. Tongue lapping here and there. Occasionally the escape of a soft slurping sound. No hesitation. No concern for dignity. No flicker of an attempt at eye contact, communication, question mark of *'Do you like it?'* He simply worked the head of Tony's cock like a true god damn dick-sucking professional.

Distantly, giddily, Tony thought it was a good thing he had jacked it twice that day, otherwise he wouldn't have lasted 2 minutes in Fontaine's mouth.

And god. He still might not.

He had to interrupt, to break Fontaine off the dizzyingly sensitive head.

"Don't *play* with it," sneered the dragon. "Are you trying to waste my time?"

He popped his dick out of Fontaine's mouth and smacked it lightly across his face. First one way, one cheek, then the other.

He held it in front of Fontaine's face, stroked it, pushed the tip rudely against his wet lips.

"Put it down your throat," Tony said.

His voice was almost unrecognizable to him. It had the droll patience of a man twice his age and a faint, almost sneering amusement. It *degraded*.

And Fontaine responded to the degradation with a visual shudder of arousal.

He didn't breathe a word — not of agreement, not of apology. He knew his input wasn't required.

Glassy-eyed, he wrapped his lips back around Tony's cock, and this time slipped past the head to begin taking the shaft.

It was still only half-hard, but grew rapidly under the ministrations of Fontaine's mouth. He *worked* it hard. Worked it with a series of deep, gulping sucks. Lips firm, head bobbing. He didn't try to use his hands to balance; he didn't need to. He was an expert. He was a man who *knew his place*.

On his knees.

Tony Jr. grew fatter, longer, more rigid, trying to stand upright. Fontaine's lips strained around it, but he showed no signs of struggle.

Tony could hardly believe the sight.

He had watched many a grown man try to choke him down, red-faced and spluttering, and been defeated. It wasn't just a question of length, but *girth*. His dick required a special strength of character, refinement of technique, and carefully planned strategy to overcome.

And yet Fontaine managed.

Tony would speculate later that it must have been a matter of sheer will... only to then conclude it was the *opposite*.

It was the total *lack* of Fontaine's will. And a complete submission to that of his Master's.

He forced it down. Swallowing. Eyes half-lidded. Nostrils flaring for breath.

And it fit.

Fontaine somehow overcame any semblance of gag reflex, opened his throat, and pushed his head forward, and Tony's fully hard eight and a quarter inches lodged in his gullet.

Fontaine's nose *brushed his stomach*.

The bliss of that all-encompassing, squeezing warmth ran up Tony's spine, into his hairline, and spiraled out into shivers that coursed through his whole body.

When the pleasure reached his hands, they sprang out as if triggered by an electric pulse.

He grabbed Fontaine's head and sank his fingers into that *perfect* silver hair. The expensive cut, the pristine styling. He raced his fingers through it, mussing it, taking a grip on it.

No resistance. No reaction. Fontaine stayed right where he was, Tony's cock burrowed and warm between his lips, filling his mouth, diving down his throat, perfectly nestled, and he let the nineteen-year-old greasemonkey *do* that, *own* his face, make a fuckhole of his mouth, because this was his nature. It was *instinct*; instinct at work in both of them. Master and servant. The dragon and the worm.

Tony's grip turned into a stroke.

Running his fingers through Fontaine's hair, zen as could be, Tony issued the command.

"Lick me."

And just like Fontaine had promised he would, Tony felt a tongue on the underside of his shaft lap forward, licking, seeking. Finding.

Fontaine sucked it all the way down his throat, deep enough to lick his balls at the same time.

He licked.

The dragon soared.

He gripped Fontaine's head again and pulled out, revealing his eight and a quarter inches spit-slimy, veiny, and throbbing. Fontaine's mouth shone, wet. Saliva on his chin.

Tony mashed his dick against Fontaine's face. He thrust, humped up against it. Sliding, grinding, over Fontaine's cheek, the side of his nose, over one set of closed eyelashes. Smearing spit.

Fontaine allowed it.

Mouth still hanging open, breath coming out heavy over his tongue, hot where it touched Tony's shaft.

Expression glassy and stupid like the screen of a broken computer.

And *flushed*. And distant, and gone, and present, and ecstatic.

Tony put the head of his cock back on Fontaine's tongue. He rubbed back and forth in the passage of his mouth — watching, waiting — and then slipped all the way back in.

And Fontaine took him with slavish gratitude.

Tony shlucked back and forth in Fontaine's mouth, his throat, watching the ecstatic flutter of his eyelids and the bulging of his cheeks.

Unreal. Unbelievable. As fantastical as Tony's dreams of flying, and yet true. Present. Ezra Fontaine. The finger-snapping, deep pockets,

C-suite exec himself. On his knees, mouth sloppy from being fucked, chin dripping wet, lips making obscene, slick sounds on every rapid stroke, his gullet doing the same. Gulping. Taking.

He allowed everything.

And Tony allowed himself to fully indulge the dragon.

Gripping Fontaine's head in both hands, he wrapped his fingers in Fontaine's *perfect*, silvering hair and he *yanked*, tugging the man forward. Shoving his hips forward to meet it, mashing Fontaine's face against his stomach. Holding him there. And, as if it were *possible* to get his dick any deeper, Tony *thrust*. With Fontaine fastened to him, lips to skin, a perfect seal. Thrusting. Pumping. Nowhere to go, but still sending his hips, his dick, forward.

The dragon was utterly serene.

This was natural, perfect, and well-earned.

Now when Tony pulled out, the once-regal man kneeling there *did* gasp for air, *did* pant loud and fast, air-starved, into the still office air. His face a mess, looking swollen and abused. One hand raised and grasping for the table edge to balance himself.

But he did not fall back, did not cough, did not wipe his mouth or his streaming eyes.

Fontaine got his balance back and immediately planted his mouth back against Tony's cock. He busily, devotedly licked the shaft, dragging his tongue up, down. Rapid. Hungry. Tender. *Wanting*. He glided his lips over the surface, sucked it. Lapped at it. Slathered it with his spit.

He looked exactly like the messy, sloppy whore Goff had claimed him to be.

Tony marveled at the sight.

I fucking did it, he thought. The sheer joy threatened to unsteady him. *I'm a fucking king. I'm a god damn god.*

No. Better.

The fucking dragonnnnn.

Before his knees could buckle, he reached behind him and hauled his boss's chair forward, dropping back down in it.

"Take my boots off," he said, playing with fire. "And my pants. And boxers."

And Fontaine obeyed.

Undoing the laces, deftly removing Tony's boots, setting them aside with a precise air as if being charged with handling a king's royal armor. Hooking his fingers in the waistband of Tony's trousers, the elastic of his boxers, hauling them down leaving him bareass, working them off over his feet. These, too, he set aside with equal care.

Naked in his zebra patterned crew socks and smudged work shirt, cock standing up nearly purple, and Ezra Fontaine kneeling in front of him, Anton 'Tony' Cargill AKA Spider Monkey AKA the motherfucking *dragon*, master of all things, came to full fucking fruition.

"Now finish your job," he said.

Fontaine did as his master bade him.

He bent down and swallowed, worked Tony's cock back down his throat in determined, hungry gulps, inch by inch. He took it all. Not easily, but with immense resolve.

Seated as if on a throne, pleasure allowed to roll and ebb freely through him now, Tony had to fight to focus. To watch the final quarter inch of his dick disappear between Fontaine's lips.

And there came that tongue again.

More now, as Fontaine focused, as he bore down and throttled himself, *licking*. Lapping at the underside of Tony's cock until reaching the very base, lapping down, finding and worshipping his balls.

Tony's eyes nearly rolled back in his head.

Fontaine choked himself harder, making throttled little sounds now, the sound of struggling air, but with no sign of backing down.

Working *harder*.

Tongue surging, striving.

Heat coursed through Tony's body, emerging from an ember that seemed to come to a boil right under the skin of his taint, and his asshole clenched violently.

He suddenly reached down, with one hand lifting his balls and pushing them towards Fontaine's mouth, with the other clamping down on the back of the man's head. Grabbing the hair. Silver. Shining. Shining like treasure.

In a final effort, Fontaine's tongue surged with a hot, sloppy urgency.

It *was* hungry. It *was* worshipful. Tony was his manna from heaven. The *Master*.

Tony held onto the back of Fontaine's head, and nutted.

And his eyes *did* roll back in his head.

It was a good thing there was no way for Fontaine to see Tony's O-face from his position, because it probably would have shattered the illusion of Tony's divinity.

Tony's fingers remained clamped down on Fontaine's head until every unwitnessed drop of cum had pumped down the man's throat, until each twitch and spasm of pleasure had passed, until his senses returned to him and his seized-up muscles finally went limp.

And he let go.

Fontaine came up with a wet, rattling drag of air. Tony's cock popped out from between his lips and he breathed heavily, drool dripping, but he still didn't gag.

For the first time since spotting the tattoo, Fontaine's eyes rose to Tony's face — not in question. His expression was still blunted. Hungry... but servile. Expectant. Not even waiting to catch his breath.

Wanting another order.

And Tony didn't know what the hell order to give him.

"Pull down your pants," he blurted out.

Fontaine reached down with a shudder. There was the clink of a belt, the rustle of fabric, the little *zzt* of a zipper.

Tony didn't know what the fuck he was going to do until he was already doing it.

He searched below with his socked foot, found the drooping-open fly and the rock-hard bulge fighting against expensive boxer fabric.

Fontaine moaned when Tony's heel bore down on him.

"You can lick my balls while you come," said Tony, his words coming out unplanned, his tone somehow exquisitely relaxed. *Truly* the Master. It was in his fucking bones.

He might have imagined that the eye contact lingered for half a second. Just a blip.

And then Fontaine sank to the level of his instincts, to the depths of subservience again, swept along on the words of his Master. He gratefully buried his face under Tony's flagging cock.

He licked and mouthed with desperate, wet hunger.

His hips pumped, his cock pulsing up and down against Tony's punishing foot. Tony pressed down harder. He twisted his foot, almost *grinding* his heel, mirroring the motion of putting out a cigarette.

Fontaine shuddered and pumped more vigorously.

He had Tony's entire left nut in his mouth, Tony's cock flopping over his head.

Something in Tony's head suddenly blinked on like a lightbulb.

He leaned forward, snatching off the desktop the very marker Fontaine had disdained before, and then he leaned down.

He yanked back Fontaine's boxers, gave the marker a single suck, and plunged the wet end inside of him.

Fontaine made a single sound against his balls.

Muffled. Ecstatic.

Tony left the marker there, sticking halfway out, and sat back in his throne.

Fontaine came.

Breath huffing fast on Tony's balls.

Exquisitely dressed, immaculately sculpted body shuddering.

Cock humping furiously against the foot which threatened to crush it. Humping, thrusting, driving until suddenly coming shorter, shallower, less so, less so.

He finished with a surprisingly quiet moan.

Discreet, thought Tony fuzzily. Easy to fuck in an alleyway. A club bathroom. Under a concrete underpass.

Tony let Fontaine stay there maybe a minute, panting and shivering and a mess, lips still pressed against Tony's sack while he struggled to catch his breath.

Then the dragon dismissed him.

"That's all," he said, the word 'worm' lingering in the tone of his voice. "Now get the fuck out."

Fontaine shakily got himself together, removed the humiliation of the marker, fixed his clothes.

And he got the fuck out.

8 THE GENERAL

Tony had no memory of leaving the garage or snagging a Taxi home, no memory of entering the back doors and getting waved in by the doorman, nor of riding the elevator up or walking into his apartment. (Okay, Goff's apartment, fuck off.)

His mind was a blank up until the moment he walked into the bedroom, sank down on the corner of the mattress, and stared spacily at the wall.

"Uh," said Jonah. "Do you mind?"

Jonah and Zelda lay all tangled up in the sheets of the guest bedroom. It was impossible to tell exactly whose limbs were where — though Zelda was clearly on top. Jonah had pulled the sheets up to obscure the real sordid details. His face was red except for where it was smeared with Zelda's lipstick; this time the shade was a very bold, middle finger to the beauty mags blue. It looked great on her. Less great on Jonah.

"He sucked my dick," said Tony.

"The silver fox?" asked Zelda.

Immediately more invested in Tony's story than whatever she had been doing with Jonah under the sheets, Zelda sat up. Titties out. She clearly did not give a shit, but Jonah gave a little yip of alarm and instinctively reached up to cover them with his hands. Protecting her modesty like human nipple pasties.

Ignoring him, Zelda leaned over and reached for the bedside bong.

Lighting it and taking a hit, she looked at Tony sitting there silently nodding his head. Nodding, nodding, nodding. Like a bobblehead.

"Well, congrats," she said. "So you're going out now?"

Tony took the offered bong and — mind still moving in slow motion — was halfway through taking a hit when her question, wafting slowly, like a falling leaf, settled in his brain.

He broke out into loserly, hacking coughs.

"Bro," said Jonah indignantly, rescuing the bong before Tony dropped it. "*Dude!*"

'*Going out?*'

Tony tried to push through the fog of recent memory, to find anything resembling clear thought, but it was like trying to hack through dense jungle with a toothbrush instead of a machete.

A jungle of lips, tongue, mouth. Fontaine's face, buried underneath his dick. The thick, sucking, choking, half-gagging-half-moaning sounds.

"Hellooo?" Someone was snapping their fingers in front of his face. "Earth to Space Monkey."

Tony blinked and looked back. "Whaguh?"

Zelda had pulled on a shirt, titties-be-gone, and Jonah had wiggled into some shorts and was the one snapping his fingers.

"What happened?" asked Jonah, curious now that nookie continuity was clearly off the table. "What, *that* good?"

"Yes." The word popped immediately out of Tony's mouth, so fervently that both Jonah and Zelda semi-cringed. "*But.*"

But.

He spilled the whole can of beans.

Not the specifics of Fontaine suckling his balls, licking him silly, obeying him like a sloppy little worm, but the discussion with his cousin. The sending of pictures. Of videos. And finally... kicking Fontaine out with his chin still wet from sucking.

"You told him get the fuck out." asked Zelda, forehead wrinkled in confusion.

"You asked your *cousin* for advice?" asked Jonah, nose crinkled in disgust.

"Listen," said Tony.

They both waited. Listening.

He didn't have shit to say.

He really had told Fontaine to get the fuck out, huh?

"What the fuck do I do now?" he finally burst out.

He groaned, leaned forward, and put his head in his hands. He yanked once at his hair in an agony of mortification, frustration. All of it.

"Shiiiiit," he moaned.

"Hey, relax." Tony felt Jonah's hand uncertainly patting his back, and heard the pit-patting, rustling sound of Zelda sliding out of bed, pulling on pants, coming around the bed. "It's gonna be okay, dude," Jonah was saying.

"Hey," came Zelda's voice. Sterner than Jonah's.

Tony looked up.

She stood in front of him, hands on hips, looking ready to deliver a lesson, but he was temporarily distracted by her shorts. They were patterned with the American flag. The blue matched her lipstick.

"Listen up," she said. "You like this guy, right?"

Was 'like' the word?

'Like' didn't seem big enough to cover the drooling, full-body, obsessive feeling that took him over.

But Tony nodded anyway. "Sure," he said.

"Then what you *need*," continued Zelda, her confidence bolstering his, "is open communication. Reciprocity. If you really want him, you can't just play kinky games. You need to tell him how you feel."

'Feel?'

Feel, beyond the *feeling* of Fontaine's velvet mouth on his nuts, the exhilarating brush of stubble against his thighs?

Tony didn't say that.

He just nodded.

And went to bed, to think about Fontaine's mouth some more.

The fully realized Dragon King perched on a spire of his conquered palace, wings half-spread for balance, talons digging deep grooves in the metal.

He regarded his kingdom as the sun began to slide down the upside-down bowl of the sky, its light turning the Dragon King into a true thing of glittering awe. Brilliant gold. Iridescent black belly.

Conquering the realm had not brought as deep a sense of satisfaction as he had expected.

It had been *far* too easy.

The legitimate rulers had gone down in a few quick, crunchy gulps, and all the noblemen and other members of the court had laid down their arms and ceased all protests immediately. They had coronated the new king while the blood of the old one still lay wet upon the glistening marble flagstones.

Dominion over these people and their silly crops was not enough.

When the Dragon King alighted from his castle's spire and flew away, it was in search of something else... something he only had an inkling of. Something he knew he would recognize upon seeing it.

And so it was.

The Dragon King found the subject of his true ambition on the warpath.

An army had come through recently and left the road like a wound, deeply worn with black dirt churned up. He passed high, high above their encampment, too high in the coming twilight to be seen, counting tents with his powerful eyes and seeking... seeking something.

He passed over the edge of the encampment and there. *There* he saw it.

A cluster of forest separated the vast camp from a small lake, and at the shoreline was a small figure.

A man.

The Dragon King tasted destiny on his tongue — hot and sweet as blood — and followed it with a hungry purr, descending into the trees.

He landed with near-complete silence despite his size, and crept through the branches of the ancient, twisted oaks until he had a perfect view of the scene.

A sensual figure stood thigh-deep in the water.

A General, based on the armor and insignia stacked carefully on a rock nearby. The armor, the insignia... and the shape of him.

Broad-backed. Muscular trunks for legs. A shapely, round ass. A sculpted chest with nipples hard from the cool air. He was heavily scarred, silver-haired and bearded, and his cock hung between his thighs flaccid but thick.

His skin was very white from traveling in full armor, but as he bent down to wash, the Dragon King caught a glimpse of deep pink between his legs. Something soft and vulnerable between the firm muscle of his buttocks.

Drool began to run hot and liquid over his tongue, between his pointed teeth and down the scales of his chin.

The General continued bathing, completely unaware he was being watched. Even his horse, tied and drowsing nearby, had noticed nothing. The Dragon King perched in perfect stealth. From that secret vantage point he watched the man touch himself. Observed the ripple of his muscles, the secrets of his naked body.

In those moments of silent, predatory appraisal, the man gradually ceased to be a general. In fact, he ceased to be a 'man' at all, but instead a concubine to be ravaged by the Dragon King, though he did not know it yet.

Finally patience abandoned him.

Branches cracked and trees crunched, shattering to the ground in a tumult of wood as the Dragon King launched himself into the air, no longer troubling himself with stealth.

The man's horse tore itself loose in a panic; before the creature could flee, the Dragon King seized it in his great talons, twisting and upending the horse with such violence that its neck snapped. It dropped, instantly limp.

Good.

There would be no beast running back to the army, alerting them to their general's danger.

The General himself had lunged for the shore, hand outstretched for his waiting blade.

Too slow.

The Dragon King hurtled towards him. He caught the General a hands-breadth from the shore, long-clawed fingers seizing him greedily around the naked waist.

The man didn't have a chance to cry out.

Clutching his prize to his chest, the Dragon King threw open his wings and took to the air, and in only seconds they had climbed higher above even the tallest and most ancient trees. The night sky graciously accepted its master, and the Dragon King slipped into a rush of wind and was gone.

And where to carry his fair concubine?

Back to the throne, the royal bedchamber?

There was no need.

The *world* was his royal bedchamber.

He landed high in the twisted mountains, in a meadow surrounded by ancient trees. A place unreachable by man, untouched and inescapable.

The King dropped his treasure onto a bed of grass and did not delay.

He swept his muzzle once up the man's naked body. Nuzzling. Relishing. Huffing the steam-hot breath of dragons against the shivering, tantalizing flesh.

Then he dropped his head to drive his tongue between the General's legs.

Seeking the soft pink delicacy he had glimpsed there before, he ploughed this way and that until the flesh suddenly yielded to him, and then plunged his tongue inside.

the General let out a hoarse cry.

Mouth still dripping wet with hunger, the King thrust his tongue deeper down the tight corridor.

His cock, risen taut against his belly, rubbed deliciously in the soft moss as he writhed.

The man let out rough, gasping shouts, one after another. "*Aah!*" He grabbed at horn, scale, anything in reach. "*Aah!*" His handsome face was flushed, distorted. His mouth moved in rhythm with the great tongue's violation, crying "Aah, aah, ahh—" with each deep inroad.

The Dragon King drew out his slavering tongue, leaving a slippery wet trail from the man's insides. The delicate entrance he had glimpsed before now stood open. It seemed to hitch and pulse, as if it were a second gasping mouth, and the King pushed his muzzle warmly against it as if to kiss.

The General let out another cry, but this one did not last.

As the Dragon King rooted between his thighs, silky muzzle and warm breath rolling over the man's sex, the shocked cry dropped and deepened to a moan.

The King continued to nuzzle, and to lick, and to give his tenderest attentions to the General's most private... vulnerable... sensitive.

And the man's clenched thighs dropped away.

His hands ceased grappling with the dragon's horns and instead hung onto them, fingers trembling, like one might cling to a lover's back.

"Prepare yourself," said the Dragon King, as hungrily nuzzled the seat of his desire, "to service your master."

"M-my master?" The proud general's mouth struggled with the word. His thighs twitched. He stared down at the King with a kind of drunken mesmer, clearly bewitched... but not *completely* under the spell. Not yet.

"I am he," said the Dragon King, raising his great head. "And you will serve me in *all things*."

He pressed forward and brought his magnificent, gleaming cock to rest upon the General's body, between the man's splayed legs.

There it throbbed, head pulsating. A clear drop welled up at the tip and then broke, spattering the General's well-muscled stomach.

"Ask me for my blessing, worm," instructed the King. "*Beg* to be my beloved slave."

He set the great, swollen head to the man's modest entrance.

The proud general *moaned* as the enormous thing thrust inside.

And he begged.

Tony awoke hurting-hard, plunged his hand down his boxers, and had jerked himself to relief before he was even fully conscious.

The dream clung to him like the wank-sweat beading on his thighs.

A sense of triumph and euphoria pervaded his still-sleepy, still-stupid mind, and the images — fleeting, scattering the way dream images often do — struck him like blowing leaves to the face.

He lay there and gazed at the ceiling.

He thought to himself: *I am the dragon.*

He thought it again, again, again, with increasing ecstasy.

I am the dragon. I am the dragon. The dragon.

I am the Dragon King!

9 SWORD AND SHIELD

"You *absolutely cannot tell* him how you feel," said Goff. "The last thing we want is EZ Ezra knowing that you're basically just a big, horny dog mindlessly humping his leg."

He pointed his coffee stirrer at Tony. "We need him to think you're the big, bad wolf."

"Right," said Tony, nodding vigorously, thinking of the Dragon King and that for once he and his cousin were on the same page. "Master of all things."

"Sure," said Goff, ignoring the weird phrasing and the weirder note in Tony's voice.

They had grabbed coffee this time. A tiny place, no seating indoor or out, just a window through which orders came in and coffees came out.

Tony couldn't tell if the literal hole-in-the-wall was peasant fare or bougie bullshit until Goff paid thirty bucks for their two coffees, handing him one. Tony gave it a suspicious sniff, hoping against rosemary and lemon zest this time.

The two of them walked down the street, under the eaves of the tall downtown buildings, where water poured over the edge in a waterfall three feet away. Goff was dressed warmly against the rain, in a heavy-gauge wool coat that should have looked like it was drowning his slight frame, but somehow didn't.

Tony was wearing running shorts and a hoodie.

He wasn't sure where they were going, or why Goff had such a sparkle in his eye about it.

Tony had called out sick — Jonah had helped with the background pukey sound effects — and assumed his cousin had done the same. But then again, *Zachary Goff* probably didn't need to 'call out' to anyone. He probably just didn't show up.

By the time Tony had finished filling him in — leaving out the dragon — Goff was grinning, eyes curved, dimples dancing on his cheeks.

"You know," remarked Goff, tossing his coffee stirrer in the river of a gutter. "I really didn't think you had it in you, 'Master of all things.'"

Tony frowned. "You didn't?"

"Not for a second," said Goff freely, affixing his coffee lid back on. "I thought you would fuck it up, big time. Ezra may be 'easy' but... well."

"What?" asked Tony, his frown becoming a glare. He didn't demand 'why would you encourage me if you thought I would fuck it up big time?' The answer to that was obvious — it would have been funny.

"Well there's 'easy,' and then there's *'easy,'*" said Goff. He noticed and acknowledged Tony's pissed face with a sparkle of the eyes, a grin as his sipped his coffee and moved on. "You might be able to push around the average soccer coach, your everyday run of the mill

DILF, but taking down a man of Ezra's resources? That's a different level."

"Resources?" Tony frowned.

"Anyway." Goff tugged up his collar as a passing car tossed water in their direction, spattering just short of Tony's exposed ankles. "Now that you've managed to make a good first impression, the real trick will be in planting your flag."

"What do you mean?" Tony danced away from the rain-spray, practically hugging the wall of the building as he followed his cousin — who walked fast for such a little dude. "'Planting my flag?'"

Goff shrugged and threw out lazy parallels. "Mark your territory. Put a ring on it. Break it to saddle."

"You mean like asking him out," Tony attempted to infer, nodding wisely.

That made Goff stop in his tracks, looking up, lip curling in faint disgust.

"Do you want a *boyfriend*, Anton?" asked Goff, dripping impatience. "Or do you want a throat goat sleeping in a dog crate at the foot of your bed, wearing a cock cage with a padlock only *you* can open?"

Tony thought that sounded *extremely* specific.

...and not like a bad time.

"Here's what we're going to do," said Goff, not waiting for an answer. "We're going to get you equipped. Once you have sword and shield in hand, and a proper set of armor on your back, the battle will be more... intuitive."

Tony could only *imagine* what he was referring to, and didn't ask. He guessed he would find out.

But the language sent a strange prickle down his spine.

Sword, shield, armor. A little bit too close to the language of his *dreams*.

He cast a suspicious, sidelong glance at his cousin. He was confident that Zachary Goff was capable of many things, but mindreading was not among them.

But if anyone in the world was capable of that, it would be *this* motherfucker, he thought.

Goff abruptly took a right and Tony hurried after him. They passed a blare of angry traffic — someone rear-ended in the busy, drenched streets — and suddenly they were in a pedestrian tunnel between buildings, Goff marching, his boots clapping briskly on the pavement, Tony's sneakers slapping.

Goff ducked right again, into an alley Tony didn't see until they were on top of it.

Tony would have been skeeved out if he'd had a chance to think about things, but he did not. Goff strode with the unlooking confidence of a man who had come this way many times before.

He stopped at an alcove in the wall, where a single door sat with no sign or light above it. The door was plain, marked only by a stained glass window. Red. Round. In the shape of a rose, Tony realized.

His cousin rapped his knuckles on the door, paused, checked his watch. He waited some specific number of seconds and then knocked again, three times, slowly.

The door opened inwards.

Tony relaxed as soon as the interior revealed itself; it was just a *shop*. A weird shop, sure, tucked away back here, but there were no bodies hanging from meathooks, no meathooks at all, in fact.

Even better, it was a *sex shop*.

Leather and lingerie mixed on racks and dangled from hangers. Dildos sat on little velvet pillows behind glass in display cases. One wall was dominated by rows of hooks, and hanging from them were assorted leather restraints — handcuffs, ankle cuffs, collars, leashes.

The walls were red, the ceiling mirrored, and off a separate hallway Tony's eyes caught on a black-painted doorway.

He took a single curious step before Goff snagged him.

"Not for you," said his cousin. "Not today."

Releasing Tony's sleeve, Goff walked on into the rows of goodies, putting his hands in his pockets and browsing with his eyes.

"You're going to want to whip him," he mulled, stopping before a rack of dangling whips. He examined them critically. "Not to be too old fashioned, but..." He smiled at Tony, dimples flashing prominent again. "Sometimes, a solid thrashing is exactly what you need to get your point across."

His words were very matter-of-fact.

"You do mean like, *consensually*, right?" asked Tony, letting his voice turn the genuine question into a joke.

"Sure," said Goff carelessly, eyes still skimming the whips. Now he reached out to touch them lightly with a single finger, one at a time, as if counting. "Riding crop, jockey whip, flogger... Do you have a preference?"

"I only ever used my hand," said Tony, flashing back on the salt-n-pepper soccer coach — and former best friend's dad, sorry Ryan — whose ass he had left purple handprints on a few months ago.

Goff gave him one of those faintly pitying, 'my cousin the caveman' looks.

"At least take your belt out next time," he said, and moved on to the next row.

They worked their way through the whole boutique that way. Goff worked fast. At some point Tony found himself holding a shopping basket, and quickly it began to fill up. Some of the stuff was recognizable... and *exciting* in the context of steely, foxy Ezra Fontaine.

A spider gag. A ball gag. Blindfolds, vibrators, clamps of all sorts, leather this-and-that's. Pretty much anything you could reasonably fit into an orifice. Some shit that even *Tony* didn't recognize. He just raised his eyebrows and did not ask.

He *did* ask, "Are you buying?" eventually, after the pile had grown absurd.

"Of course," said Goff. "My treat. It's your birthday soon, right?"

"Umm." Tony eyed the pile. "Not really."

Goff dismissed that with a quick wave. They had finally come to the final row, and he turned to Tony, turned to riffle through the basket with lips moving as if counting, making sure they had everything.

"You won't need all of this, of course," said Goff. "And some of it is probably a little... ambitious for you."

Tony scowled.

"But," Goff went on, plucking out a gag and toying with its band, eyes narrowing to double-check the quality. "I want you to have the *best* shot at winning Ezra over."

Tony wasn't an idiot.

He was cock-stupid sometimes, but at this relatively unhorny moment, he felt his instincts prodding at the inside of his guts, saying 'Hey, dear cousin Zachary *maybe* doesn't have your best interests at heart.'

Not that Tony needed to be *told*. He'd known since childhood that people from *that* side of the family were snakes.

But Goff's enthusiasm now made him wonder *exactly* what was motivating his cousin. He wondered if *maybe*. Possibly. Things had not ended well with him and Fontaine before.

Tony did not ask.

Instead he asked, "When exactly am I going to *use* all this?" as they stood at the checkout, where an impassive man with flamingos on his tie ran the items through.

"Oh, don't worry," said Goff gaily. "Soon enough."

His dimples winked ominously.

10 KRAV MAGA

Tony ran on the treadmill, bouncing along on his relatively new sneakers, which had just reached the breaking-in sweet spot — cushy support without the threat of arch pain.

Running in place... it was a good representation of how he felt. Trapped, almost. Like something was *gaining* on him. Like in dreams, where you try to run away and find your legs stuck, your motion gooey and slow, and you go nowhere.

That was him.

But Tony tried to focus on the positives — cushy shoes, cushy shoes — and not the fact that he was having his little jog *at the exclusive men's health club frequented by Ezra Fontaine.*

Complete with antigravity treadmills, sauna, solarium, and rooms where personal trainers were coaching the 'who's who' of the preening upper echelon of their city.

Goff had gotten him in, of course.

Tony hadn't even thought to question Goff's knowledge of the place or ability to get in, but he *did* think to question his cousin's apparent knowledge of Fontaine's schedule.

'Thought' being the key word. Tony had not asked.

He had been too busy screaming internally after Goff told him that Fontaine had *Krav Maga* with a trainer at seven, and would hit the showers after that, and that Tony had better get in quick, and—

And then Tony had interrupted with, "Hey, fucking excuse me, but did you say Krav Maga?"

And Goff had sneered. "Afraid?"

Afraid of what? That Fontaine was going to react to a grabby teenager popping into his shower with a throat strike?

If Fontaine had not already drooled all over his cock and debased himself over the phone — Twice! — Tony would have peaced out.

Because yeah, he was tall. He was pretty built for his age. The garage and home gym had both put some polish on his muscles. But he didn't know fucking *Krav Maga*.

Tony had plenty of time to think, jogging along, waiting for the pivotal hour to roll around, long enough that he nearly decided to hop off the treadmill and go check out that sauna. With every passing minute the plan felt more absurd. What was he *doing*, really?

And then he caught sight of a flash of silver hair.

His stomach turned over.

He whipped his head around, nearly crashing off the treadmill, slapping the emergency stop button just in time.

His glimpse of Fontaine lasted only a moment, and he only knew it was Fontaine because, well, he *knew*. Deep in his soul.

The silver-haired figure emerged from one of the private rooms and was gone in two paces, down a hall, in the direction of the showers.

Tony swallowed hard.

He looked at his time on the treadmill screen without seeing it. And then his eyes drifted down, fell to the hefty black gym bag on the floor.

The showers and changing room were largely empty. The exclusivity of the club naturally kept membership down and traffic low, and this time of day seemed unpopular. Tony imagined most of the crème de la crème member base was out on the town at this hour. Boozing, schmoozing. Swapping business cards and gossip.

Water was running in only one of the shower stalls.

The warm, steady flow of it beckoned Tony, who trailed down the changing room aisle in an almost hypnotized state.

He carried the hefty waterproof bag over one shoulder, held his bundle of clothes and towel under the other arm.

The open shower doors showed spacious stalls, each with a little bench inside. No space under the dividing walls, just over the top. Bottles of complimentary shampoo, body wash, conditioner lined up under every showerhead.

The single closed door was made of cloud glass. Steam clouded it even further.

But Tony could make out the dim shape of a figure inside.

His trepidation fell away with each item of clothing he discarded.

By the time Tony was naked, he was ready.

He opened the door, stepped inside, and closed it behind him.

Ezra Fontaine looked up from under the shower.

At the sight of him standing there steaming, his hair wet, water streaming over him, all the questions and uncertainty boiling in Tony's brain went quiet. Still.

He gazed, transfixed, at the water flowing over Fontaine's body.

His body...

Tony had obviously known that Fontaine would be naked when he walked in — it was a fucking shower — but that knowledge had somehow dropped off his radar, far behind all the other boiling thoughts.

Now he looked at Fontaine in three-quarters profile. A muscled, perfected profile. *Tirelessly* sculpted. Broad shoulders. Big, round pecs rising off his chest. Flat, hard-muscled stomach. Gorgeous, firm peach of an ass perched at the peak of his powerful thighs.

Marked.

Almost more startling than his sheer naked reality was that which Tony had glimpsed in pictures and video — the piercings. The ink.

The golden, ruby-tipped barbells through his nipples.

A matching golden ring through the head of his cock.

And one he hadn't glimpsed at all before — a little slip of gold piercing his navel.

The piercings should have been the most remarkable things on Fontaine's body, but they weren't.

What was more shocking were the tattoos.

They weren't like biker tats, or any style Tony recognized, but instead a rough, grotesque assembly of words. Some were small, unreadable without bending down close. Some were large, screaming at him.

They said:

SLUTHOLE. COCKWHORE. FUCKTOY.

Tony didn't think on them.

He simply absorbed the image, the *complete* image of the man, the fox, the c-suite cutthroat. And the 'cutthroat' gazed back at him without a whisper of that sharp, icy air, none of the 'too good for this' attitude. Fontaine's face was open.

Tony had had some abstract thoughts of permission. Consent. Of waiting for a sign.

Now that he was before the man himself, those abstractions dissolved.

He put his bag down on the small bench and he went, hand casually outstretched, *knowing* that Fontaine would let himself be touched, that any part of the man's body was literally and figuratively up for grabs.

And he scooped a hand between Fontaine's legs to grasp him by the balls. Nestling for just a moment, then closing his fingers tight. Drawing him *firmly* out from under the water and close enough to feel.

To feel, full body.

He pressed himself, naked and dry, against the naked and wet Fontaine. Crudely holding him one-handed between the legs as if by a leash. With his other hand gathering their cocks together. Sliding them alongside each other, parallel.

"Look," he said.

Fontaine dropped his gaze to look at what Tony wanted him to see.

The contrast.

Fontaine was not small. He had a good six inches on him.

But even limp, Tony was a *freak*.

Longer.

Thicker.

Side by side it was no competition. No question at all.

"You remember your Master?" asked a cool voice.

It came from Tony's lips... but it was the voice of the dragon.

It was the dragon who thrust his fat dick up against Fontaine's dwarfed one. Frotting. Gloating.

A shiver went through Fontaine's body, unmistakable. The glazed cast had come over his eyes. Tony could feel Fontaine's soul shrinking, and his own growing, and he *stared* — his eyes making their blatant way up and down — at the shining wet, the *bare*, gropable, grabbable, takeable vulnerability of Fontaine's naked self, reading 'SLUTHOLE' and 'FUCKTOY.'

And his eyes finally settled on Fontaine's cock.

Fat, but flaccid. Dispirited. Adorned with that impressively big ring. Beautiful, but cowed.

He wanted to bring it to life. See it bulging and twitching with need.

He wrapped his fingers around it.

Fontaine's mouth fell open, though he made no sound, as Tony began not to rub, but to *pull*. Long, firm, dragging strokes, like he was trying to stretch the thing out.

With one hand still keeping its vise-grip on Fontaine's balls, Tony gave the object of his obsession the rough, punishing treatment he had fantasized about.

It wasn't about hurting.

It was about seeing that expression on *Ezra Fontaine's face.*

The lips parted, semi-shock, semi-pleasure, semi-flinch on each *rough* tug between his legs.

And it was about the lack of protest.

The walking in unannounced.

The grabbing. Touching.

And Fontaine the immaculate, the lofty, the feared exec, standing there *getting hard* at the rough treatment, flinching and getting *hard*, coming alive and erect in Tony's hands, and outside the indistinguishable chatter of other people, people who maybe knew him, who would have been shocked to see him going glassy-eyed and servile.

And the way Tony uncurled one finger from gripping the man's balls and stroked its tip down over his hole, and in the midst of the pain and the shame and the need for discretion, the thick, rich, muscular, more-than-twice-his-age CEO *moaned* and dropped his head onto Tony's shoulder.

Yeah.

That was it.

That's what life was about: sinking barely your fingertip into a man whose net worth probably exceeded most cities' spending budget, and hearing him softly, *helplessly* groan *"Master."*

Tony knew then that he didn't need the bag of accessories his cousin had hooked him up with. He was, after all, the fucking *dragon*. He didn't need a leash and collar to prove his mastery over his servant.

But he fastened the collar around Fontaine's neck anyway.

Clipped the leash on.

Wrapped the leash once around his thigh, the excess around his hand, and held Fontaine's mouth captive between his legs with about two inches of leeway in any direction.

The dragon sat on the bench with one leg up, draped casually over Fontaine's back, and he got his ass eaten better and deeper than ever before in his life.

When he fed some slack into the leash, Fontaine moved to the insides of his thighs, to his balls, up over his cock to suck at his *belly button*, the whole time *worshipping*. Licking, kissing, trailing spit. Ravenous. Drunk. Submissive. *Desperate* to submit. Following anywhere that Tony led his mouth. *Anywhere.*

Tony dreamed about having this at home. Having this chained, naked to his bed, and every night sliding under the sheets to a hot, wet mouth looking for something to suck. Every morning waking to the sensation of a tongue bathing his balls, his cock, his ass. Letting that tongue wake him up, get him hard, and then...

Tony paused in his dreaming and let slack glide into the line.

Fontaine instantly understood, as if Tony had projected the idea into his mind.

Fontaine stopped his slobbering and slid down, slid all the way to the floor and the end of the leash. And there he turned around.

He presented himself *just* as he had in the mirror at the tailor shop.

Resting on elbows and knees. Face down — spare shower droplets dripping onto the back of his head. Back smoothly arched. Ass up — ready to be fucking demolished. *Begging* to be fucking demolished. Thighs apart. Pierced cock hanging down between them, stiff and flushed with blood. Its golden ring gleaming.

But Tony could see more clearly now than he had in the shop.

Scrawled all across Fontaine's naked back were names.

Not just names... but signatures.

Different handwriting. Some faded. Many clearly in the process of being removed, but others looking like the result of clumsy handling of a tattoo gun. None were fully readable. Tony thought he caught snippets of a few legible pieces. *'Tom.' 'David.' 'Turner.'*

He thought of graffiti on concrete overpasses. *'Big Dick T-Bone Was Here.'*

Tony trailed first his eyes, then his fingertip down Fontaine's back. Tracing them. Counting.

Fontaine was still. Silent.

Knowing what Tony saw. Awaiting his judgment.

Counting.

Finally concluding: Forty-three.

What came to Tony's mind wasn't judgment, or pity, but a sudden flash of humor.

'SLUTHOLE, COCKWHORE, FUCKTOY' was right.

11 KISS

Fontaine hadn't moved an inch during the entire inspection.

He was as still — and as perfectly put together — as an enormous sex toy.

Tony cupped his ass.

He skimmed one thumb down, inward, to brush over Fontaine's ready entrance.

A shiver went through the man's body. Tony felt it — The anticipation? The arousal? — pulse under his thumb.

Did Fontaine really expect a full-on plowing? Right here, right now? Did he intend to clench his teeth and endure his new Master's every inch, to serve as the 'fuckhole' his tattoos proclaimed him, with no expectations of anything but submitting to the dick of whoever was on top of him?

Tony moved his thumb, knelt down, and pressed a long lick between his legs.

The spasm that went through Fontaine felt more like shock than pleasure.

He began to lift his head, his front end, and Tony gave a sharp pop on the leash. Immediately Fontaine sank obediently back down.

Tony cupped Fontaine's ass in both hands, spread it, and *spat*, once, loud as a gunshot in the now-quiet locker room.

He watched the spit trickling down Fontaine's taint for a moment, threatening to drip off, and at the last moment bent to gather it on his tongue again. He spread it slowly back upwards, painting a trail.

And he wormed his way back up, found the shivering spot again with his tongue, and went to *work*.

Fontaine submitted only with twitches. Gasps. The occasional hoarse sound, somewhere between a whine and a moan.

Tony gathered that the man had been fucked a lot — like, *a lot* a lot — but very rarely had his ass eaten.

Tony regretted he didn't have the proper amount of time to dedicate to slopping Fontaine silly — two straight hours felt like a good place to start — but he put in his A game. Went for the gold. Shot for the moon. And didn't surface until the thick-muscly, grown ass man under him had turned to quivering jelly.

Straightening up, Tony gauged his work by pressing the head of his cock against Fontaine's hole and gliding back and forth. It was, he noted proudly, slippery as fuck.

He propped himself up behind the spit-shiny, quivery hunk of ass, and again spread it with his hands.

Fontaine exhaled, arched his back, and pushed back towards him, giving. Offering. Expecting.

And what Tony gave him was a modest chunk of swiftly lubed-up silicone.

It *was* a dildo — plucked from Goff's bag of tricks — and no practice size, either, but it was no Tony.

It slipped inside with an ease that made Tony *groan*, and salivate.

Fontaine took the first three inches with no movement, nothing but a barely perceptible exhale, and for a moment Tony just sat back on his heels and took in the view. Stroking himself. Looking at the older man spread, bent, *penetrated*.

He pulled it back, pushed it in. Back, forth. A little deeper. Watched its thickening girth start to sink in more easily, watched the man's body yielding to it, opening, heard the soft exhale of effort.

Tony almost had to stop and wonder why the fuck he was torturing himself.

If he had been *just* Tony, he would have said 'all right, that's plenty of foreplay,' tossed the dildo aside. And gone in pounding.

But the masterful, *reptilian* knowledge of the dragon had more patience than that.

Patience enough to move in behind Fontaine, to *nearly* fuck, but instead push his painfully rigid cock down between the man's thighs, against and then aligned with Fontaine's own severe hard-on.

Patience enough to brace the base of the dildo against his stomach, so that *as* he thrust his hips forward, *as* he drove his cock upon Fontaine's, *as* their bodies clapped together, the dildo pushed simultaneously deeper in the exact same rhythm.

It wasn't fucking, a voice in Tony's head protested.

But the dragon bent over Fontaine's back, reaching under to gather his servant's balls in hand once more, and took a secure grip. Fingers mercilessly tight around the base of his cock. And the dragon began thrusting.

And the dragon made Fontaine come three times.

And when the dragon finally let up, and sat back against the wall, taking a breather for himself, Fontaine could barely move from his spot on the floor.

But he did.

Entire body shaking, looking like a man clawing his way out of a seizure state, the rich, gorgeous, classy Ezra Fontaine came on all fours. Collapsed at the dragon's heel. Mouthed his heel. Might have been trying to kiss it, or suck it. Mouthed up the arch of his foot, his ankle, his calf. Made his way up the leg like that, kissing, licking, exhausted, slack-jawed and dull-eyed, to reach the throbbing of his master.

He finally closed his lips around it with a muffled groan.

Sheer sound of desperation.

He took Tony down his throat, not sucking but *swallowing*, as if his need for Tony's cum had escalated to the level of literal starvation.

And Tony nearly gave it to him.

He *wanted* to give it to him.

But for some reason Tony was suddenly compelled to fight the hot-cold zigzags in his spine, the trembling in his extremities, to not come down Fontaine's *gorgeous*, bulging throat.

He pulled himself free with a wet pop and a gasp from Fontaine's mouth, and before a full thought could form, he had bowled the fine, expensive older man over onto his back and pushed his legs open.

Tony bore down between his legs like an animal, cockhead *kissing* his hole. Feeling the warmth, the slick of lube, sensing the squeezing heat within.

And Fontaine let his thighs fall apart, wide and recipient. Throat working, gulping. Mouth panting. Loud, ready panting. Anyone could have heard them now.

Tony plunged his fingers inside.

He felt Fontaine contract upon them, heard the shocked gasp, moan, and then *YELP* as Tony began to thrust, roughly, fingers scissoring.

Fontaine gazed up just as Tony had always imagined him.

Mouth open, no longer able to hold back any sound, all but *crying* for breath, for respite, for more. A scarlet flush painting him from throat to chest. Legs spread, hips open. All his muscles trembling from overuse. Nothing cool, suave, sneering, about him. Collared. Slut. Thoroughly surrendered. Allowing.

Tony came against Fontaine's ass, right where his fingers were roughly fucking. And he finger-fucked it inside. Coming in bursts, little explosions going off behind his eyes. Panting and wheezing, groaning, wringing himself out, *pouring* himself onto the entrance. Using his cum like so much lube.

Fontaine looked on, moaning in the rhythm of Tony's thrusting fingers.

And then when Tony had finished — when he sat back on his heels, panting, mind reeling — Fontaine reached down for the hand still absently toying at the edge of him.

Fontaine took Tony's wrist, sat up, and slipped the fingers directly between his lips.

He sucked. His lips firm, warm. His mouth hungry.

He sucked each finger clean and then licked Tony's palm, scouring every drop of cum.

Tony watched through a daze.

He didn't move until Fontaine had finished, had let go of his hand.

And with the same hand Tony suddenly seized him by the collar, dragged him forward, kissed his mouth.

Kissed him just as hungrily as Fontaine had sucked up his cum, but more *aggressively*. Wrapping his other hand around the back of Fontaine's head. Holding hard, gripping his hair, and trying to shove his entire tongue into Fontaine's mouth.

It was a spitty, hint-of-cum flavored mess.

He finally let go, released Fontaine, and fell back to sit on the tiles again. Trying to *finally* catch his breath.

They were both silent.

Well.

They were both incredibly *noisy*, the way they painted, but neither of them *said* anything.

And gradually... as Tony's breath returned to him... so too did his brain.

Holy shit.

The thought came to him colored first with euphoria. Then with near horror.

He hesitated, nearly *flinched*, before he could bring himself to lift his eyes again, to look at Fontaine.

The man.

The *mess*.

Fontaine lay there sticky, shaky, breathless. It was like someone had taken the cold, sharp figure of Ezra Fontaine, corporate cutthroat, and put him through a sex blender. His lips were swollen. His hair was *fucked*, falling over his forehead unrecognizable from its usual meticulous style.

And the situation between his legs... well, it was unspeakable.

Hot as *fuck*, but unspeakable.

He looked like he'd had a train run on him.

The idea delighted Tony in one heartbeat, thinking with pride of his fine toy-fucking and finger-fucking technique, and horrified him in the next. It was like he had taken a— a— a whatever-the-fuck, a Ming vase, and exploded it with his dick. *Surely* there had to be repercussions.

Pride might have overcome horror if not for the strangeness on Fontaine's face.

The way that he lifted his fingers shakily to his lips, touching them, as if reflecting on what had just happened.

The *kiss*.

Grabbing a hot older man by the hair, by the ass, by the cock and balls, dragging him around and fingering him, ramming him with a dildo, ramming a dick down his throat, that was all fine and good, thought Tony, but kissing?

It just...

Well, it wasn't very *draconic*, was it? It wasn't reptilian. It wasn't grab you by the dick make you suck and swallow *dominant*, was it?

Tony could still taste it.

Impulsively he wiped his mouth, pushed himself up from the ground, and wordlessly stepped past the thoroughly debauched Fontaine. He stepped under the water and, without so much as a glance downward, stole a squirt of the complimentary body wash and gave himself a quick once-over scrub. Rapidfire wash, rinse, done. Don't look down. Don't acknowledge. Play it cool.

The rising tide of 'Why the *fuck* did you do that?' in his head had begun to rise to a high wail when he finished, and he just *fled*.

Well, he power-walked out. Long, confident strides. Head high.

Leaving his bag of goodies and all behind.

As soon as the clouded glass door was closed behind him, Tony dropped all pretense of calm. He grabbed his towel, leapt into his clothes still dripping-wet, and abandoned the changing room like there was a bomb about to go off inside. He passed the antigravity treadmills. The spa doors. He passed the cheerful attendant at the front desk who said, "Have a great night, sir," and Tony acknowledged him with an incoherent jumble of not-words.

All the while thinking, '*Why?*' as the mental image of Fontaine's blank expression, touching his lips, played in Tony's mind on repeat.

Why had he listened to his god damn cousin?

Why had he thought that the subterfuge of sneaking into Fontaine's gym was a good idea?

And why the fuck had he kissed him?

12 THE CONCUBINE

Tony cracked open a bottle of Penguin filtered alpine and stood in the rectangle of light from his fridge, in his otherwise dark kitchen. City lights barely infiltrated the windows at this height; there was only a slight hint of a glow. Otherwise, just stars outside. Well. A few of them. The handful that light pollution allowed to show.

He chugged the water in three enormous gulps, then tossed the bottle in the sink. It clattered amongst the heaped recyclables.

For a moment, it seemed like the high pile would remain stable — and then it collapsed.

Empty bottles of Penguin water scattered all over the kitchen floor.

Tony put his hands on his hips.

He stood there for many long minutes, considering picking them up. Considering a lot of things. Considering whether he was going to go to work in the morning. Considering whether he was going to barge into the guest bedroom and either wake up or interrupt Jonah and Zelda, ask them for advice. Considering.

His hair was still wet. Rain outside — and his lack of preparation, not carrying an umbrella — had kept it from drying.

He glanced at his phone, at the text message his cousin had sent him about an hour ago. It read:

How did it go?

Tony squinted at the text with fresh, just-cummed-then-walked-in-several-blocks-of-rain clarity.

Okay, question.

Why would Goff care?

He took it as an ominous sign.

Zachary Goff was not exactly a generous spirit at heart. His investment here was *not* because he wanted his baby cousin to get his dick wet and find happiness. Tony didn't even think that the investment was about their previously established deal at this point. Goff didn't care *this* much about whether or not he played greasemonkey.

So what was it?

Tony thought that he probably didn't want to know.

Tony didn't respond to the text.

He didn't go bother Jonah and Zelda, either.

He imagined they were probably all cuddled up at this point. Wearing each other's clothes. Snoozing. Or smooching.

He kicked moodily at an empty water bottle on his way out of the kitchen. (He missed.)

He meandered down the hall, chucked off his clothes, and flopped facefirst into his bed wet hair and all.

Sleep came fast — as it often did after nutting so hard you went temporarily deaf — and the dreams grabbed hold.

The palace of the Dragon King was opulent, but that opulence stopped dead at the mouth of the dungeon's passage, which lay like a black gullet at the base of a vast stairway.

The Dragon King slithered down the passage, tail trailing behind him, needing no torch to light his way.

The gold of his eyes gleamed like twin spectres in the vast cavern.

At the very bottom of the pit — after dozens of twists and turns and side passages — lay the set of metal bars, the smell of iron. The smell of warm human flesh. The sound of chains rustling, clinking, as their prisoner heard (or sensed) the coming of the master of all things.

the Dragon King spat flame onto the nearby torchheads, and light fell in a golden plume over the General.

The General clambered up to a standing position on his metal cot. A set of manacles originating from each side and connected to each wrist, prevented him from launching himself off the bed or doing anything more fierce than baring his teeth.

He did not snarl 'beast,' or 'away with you!' or any number of other barbs which the Dragon King would have anticipated from lesser men.

The man simply fastened his icy eyes upon his captor in baleful recognition.

The Dragon King leered. He coiled himself comfortably against the bars, eyes raking the General's bare body. Pleased with its strength. Its poise. Pleased by the marks of his own love-making, the mating cuts upon waist and thigh.

"Are you ready to succumb to your fate?" asked the Dragon King.

The General made no reply, only lifted his lip in what seemed an involuntary disdain. The Dragon King thought that might be his only response — as it had been the past several days — but then the man spoke.

"Others have tried to hold me captive," he said, and the Dragon King was delighted to hear a note of ego he hadn't expected from the stoic, humbly appearing man.

"You think I will succumb to *your* tortures?" asked the General, and this time the note of pride was prominent.

The marks of those old tortures were upon him; paler than the fresh love scrapes, they climbed his body from bottom to top. Old burns. The distinctive discoloration — almost silver — of a warlock's scepter.

"Have I tortured you?" asked the Dragon King.

The General made no response, but his face — pale from the dungeon's chill — suddenly seemed to color.

The Dragon King's reptilian lips stretched in a grin.

He sent the tip of his tail crawling through the bars, a long, sinewy black and gold tentacle that crept across the stone floor and climbed the bed to touch the General's ankle.

The man shuddered as the tail — warm with internal draconic flame — twined up his leg, wrapping around muscular calf and thigh to nudge the already stiffening shaft of his cock.

"Is this torture?" asked the Dragon King.

His captive general said nothing, only shuddered as that thin, prehensile tip coiled warmly around his shaft and began its gentle squeezing. Rippling. The same muscular rippling as a snake around its prey.

"You needn't live in this squalor," coaxed the Dragon King. He sent the tip of his tail further on, the length of it sliding in the dust, the clever end of it slipping between the General's legs. "You know I would make an honorable concubine of thee."

The man did not resist the penetration, no more fiercely than he had resisted the King's advances before. There was no sound of protest, only the expulsion of a single hot breath, clouding in the cool air. Then... a very soft groan.

The Dragon King slowly worked deeper into him, tail filling, thickening. The General's insides were hot and squeezing. They pulsed, throbbed as the tail coaxed and rubbed promisingly.

The Dragon King pressed his massive body against the bars, the black iridescence of his belly gleaming under candlelight, and let his cock slip from its sheath to reach for the object of its desire.

The General saw it, and he groaned.

He was strong against torture, perhaps. Stoic in the face of *pain*. He was a strong man.

But dignity could not defeat the desire that betrayed itself in his expression.

The Dragon King curled his talons around the metal bars... and pushed them aside. The bars — thick as a man's thigh — gave instantly to his strength, bending and then breaking one at a time until the great reptilian lord could course through the gap.

The General gave no protest as he was overcome, gathered up, as the Dragon King effortlessly snapped his chain and then drew the man into the warmth of his coils.

When he brought the man to straddle his belly, pressed to his great, throbbing cock, the General only curled himself around the heat.

The Dragon King withdrew his tail and pushed his long, eager member into the clutching embrace between his captive's legs.

No... pain would not break this noble human spirit.

Only pleasures of the flesh would tame him.

Dragon King and petty human worm, Master and servant, they coiled and fornicated, grunting their pleasure. Hissing. Groaning. The fresh cut of talons rose upon the General's flesh, striping his muscular buttocks, his thighs, the places where his Master gripped and held him fast. The man's human sex throbbed, rigid and pink, paling almost to white in contrast against the dragon's black belly. It bobbed as he moved with the compulsive rigors of their joined heat — his hands braced flat upon his Master's scales, his hips rising and thrusting down, his mouth fallen open in great pants of bliss.

Finally, the General gave a cry.

Surrender.

The Dragon King blew out the torches.

He carried his captive through the cold dark of the dungeons up into the light, into the first tier of his palace where he threw his wings wide open and took flight. Spiraling up through the enormous atrium, he shot towards the patch of bloodred evening sky overhead. At the very top — having passed floors of statuary, libraries, great halls, all gleaming flashes of kingly wealth — he drew shut his wings with a snap, a *crack* in the air, and landed upon a raised dais.

The dais was solid gold and deeply scarred from a thousand landings, its polished surface rent by the King's enormous talons.

All around them were wistfully swaying aspen trees, soft grass, lush ferns — the rich verdancy of a forest. The palace roof had been made so at the dictates of its ruler. Here he slept, reclined in the luxury of pure sun, and here he perched on the edge and overlooked his kingdom, his eyes seeing far. Seeing all.

An artificial stream trickled by. It was lined with a bed of moss, upon which he lay his conquered General.

The man, weak from captivity and the rigors of their coupling, did not rise. He touched the moss with fingers that trembled slightly.

The Dragon King saw the man's eyes follow the treeline, rise to the red sky, trace its bloody color to the deepening purple in the east.

"Here I have brought you," said the King, "and here you will remain. But..." His steaming breath flared in the cooling night air. "...will you remain as slave-worm, or treasured concubine? The choice is yours."

His low, dark laughter brought with it a deep, dark night.

Only he — golden sovereign — gleamed still.

Gleamed with the richness of a star.

13 GRUMPY GUS

Tony didn't set an alarm.

He didn't call into work, either.

His brain — not usually exactly laden with deep thoughts — was one hundred percent stuffed to capacity. It was *bubbling*. Boiling over. There was no way he could handle even making an excuse to Mayhew, let alone looking at the inside of an engine and saying 'hm, this is your problem, that's a rubber chicken,' or whatever the hell mystery might roll into the shop.

He slept until noon. He might have slept longer through sheer will, desperate to *not* think, if Jonah hadn't busted in.

Jonah sprang to the bedside and, swaying from side to side to some internal music, bounced his hands on Tony's asscheeks like playing a bongo drum.

"Wake up," he sang. "Wake up, wake upppp, there are dinosaur pancakes."

Tony turned his head to squint at Jonah with one reproachful eye.

"What are dinosaur pancakes?" he muffled through the pillow.

"It's a surprise," said Jonah, still merrily bongoing Tony's butt. "Come on, fuckbucket. Uppy up."

Dinosaur pancakes turned out to be not, as Tony would have guessed, pancakes in the shape of dinosaurs.

They were instead regular-shaped pancakes filled with Fruity Pebbles and chunks of banana. Zelda's specialty, it turned out.

Tony sat at the table looking at his stack of rainbow-speckled pancakes, plated with a healthy swizzle of whipped cream, a scattering of sprinkles, and one beautifully fanned strawberry.

Zelda and Jonah were not gross enough to handfeed each other or do googoo gaga eyes over the table, like some new couples, but their version of new couple bliss was almost more annoying. They talked constantly and animatedly about the shared interests they'd turned out to have in common; namely, DnD, mycology, and renaissance fairs.

Eyeing them as he forked around his pancakes, Tony thought moodily that you would have expected cooler from a combination whose combined hotness quotient was objectively through the roof.

"What's with the sourpuss, grumpy gus?" Zelda asked him, poking the air with her fork at him.

"Don't call me a grumpy gus."

"What's with the sourpuss, sulky bitch?"

Jonah chortled through a mouthful of dinosaur pancakes.

"You want to know?" Tony finally demanded, stirred to true grumpiness now.

"Yes," they chorused, like the awful in-sync couple they had become.

"I kissed him," he said.

They swapped a look. Zelda's singular raised eyebrow asked 'Is that bad?' and Jonah's doubly raised eyebrows said 'Yikes!'

Finally they both turned back to him.

"So?" asked Zelda.

'*So?*' indeed.

Tony fidgeted with his phone, thinking of the *very* explicit text chain between him and Ezra Fontaine, and about the total silence since they had met in person.

Tony was nowhere articulate enough to articulate his feelings, so instead he forked at his dinosaur pancakes and said simply:

"I don't think he liked it."

"Did he say that?" asked Jonah, just as Zelda butted in, "Did you ask him?"

"No," said Tony to both, feeling himself go extra scowly at their, what, basic logic? They didn't *get* it. Men like Ezra Fontaine, you didn't just '*ask* him' things. It was either jam your dick down his throat to stop him questioning the situation, or perish.

"You should ask," said Jonah, with an obnoxious air of insight. Like he was the fucking grandmaster of romance now that he had locked down a girlfriend. "What if he did like it?"

"Yeah." Zelda bopped her fork affirmingly in the air, and added, "He might ask you to do it again."

Now they both gave Tony a significant look, eyebrows wiggling, in a way that made it clear that by 'do it' they meant more than just kissing.

Tony was contemplating giving them a more detailed summary of what went down — put them off their pancakes and knock them off their *smug* romantically fulfilled pedestal — when the doorbell rang.

"Not it," said Jonah immediately.

"Nor I," said Zelda.

"Neither of you officially fucking live here," said Tony, sour as lemon, and he pushed away his dinosaur pancakes and went to answer the door.

There stood two couriers. Each stood facing straight forward as if trying to ignore the other, each with a somehow miffed air about them, like Tony had been trying to secretly juggle two dates and accidentally scheduled them at the same time.

"Anton Cargill?" said one — the one on the left — promptly as Tony opened the door.

The one on the right looked silently pissed he hadn't said it first. He tacked on, "Anton Cargill, also known as *Tony?*" which was just over the top, but seemed to serve the purpose of one-upping the first courier.

"Uh," said Tony. "Yeah."

He heard the sound of scraping chairs behind him and knew that Zelda and Jonah were both poking their head around the corner to see what was up.

"Package for you," said the 'also known as *Tony*' tryhard, holding up said package, and Tony noted with a suppressed snort that both of their couriers' packages were the same small size, though this one was wrapped in dark red paper and the other in simple brown.

"Great," said Tony, and held out both hands, one to each courier.

Both paused. They didn't *quite* exchange glares. That would have been unprofessional.

But they glanced sharply, once, out of the corners of their eyes, in each other's direction as they wordlessly handed him the paper-wrapped packages. Light, Tony noted. Probably not a bomb or something like that inside. Or a dildo. And those were the two possibilities that came immediately to Tony's mind. Beyond that, it was a mystery.

"Have a fantastic day, sir," said one courier, just as the other said, "Have an *excellent* day, sir," and then both *did* look daggers at each other.

Tony closed the door in their faces before he could be witness to courier-on-courier crime.

Bringing his packages to the abused coffee table, Tony set them down and sank onto the sofa, where he regarded them with crossed arms.

Almost immediately he had Zelda and Jonah on either side of him.

"Plain one first, I think," said Zelda, sounding like a royal advisor counseling on some serious matter. "Always the best for last, right?"

"Well, we don't know which is best until we open them," pointed out Jonah, also sounding annoyingly wise, crossing his arms in a mirror of Tony's consideration. His head was nodding thoughtfully.

Tony rolled his eyes at the high ceiling and grabbed package number one.

He ripped off the plain paper, letting it fall crunchily to the floor, and popped open the little wooden box. Inside the box, velvet-lined, was a gleaming engraved nameplate. It read:

ANTON G. CARGILL

"Oh, very nice," approved Jonah, then paused. "What's it for?"

Tony could imagine.

He opened the note that lay neatly folded underneath, and read it out loud.

"'For your new office. Since things are going so well. Looking forward to welcoming you to the team. Yours, cousin Zachary.'"

"Shit," said Jonah under his breath.

'Shit' was right, thought Tony.

Something about it felt almost threatening. The fact that it was engraved. *Cut* into. Permanent. The sharp brilliance of the metal. Goff had put it together so quickly, too. How had he *known* about things going well? Had he guessed? Or did he have spies in the men's health club, jotting down notes for him about who was or wasn't fucking in the showers?

Tony put down the nameplate with a strong sense of unease.

Well *that* package made sense, he thought.

But he couldn't imagine what the hell would be in the other.

He tore away the paper — letting it settle to the floor with the rest, red and brown mingling like fall leaves — and found a *very* similar box. Wooden. Velvet lined.

However, inside was not a nameplate and a note, but a little plush cushion with a single playing card on top.

Tony plucked it up, found it surprisingly heavy, and turned it around.

One side showed the Ace of Spades.

The other side was plated with solid gold.

On it was engraved, in neat calligraphy: ADMIT ONE. Underneath that was an address.

Tony didn't know the exact place, but he knew the street; it was *the* center of upper echelon clubbing in town. He'd never been able to get into some of them, even when he had cash to flash.

Now, he realized why.

You needed a golden ticket.

And he had one.

Puzzled, he put down the card and picked up the small stiff-paper square of a note which had come with it.

He skimmed it with a frown, and then his heart flip-flopped dramatically at the signature.

He made a strange squeaky noise.

Jonah whipped it out of his hand to read, then said "*Ooooooh*," in a delighted, half-mocking voice, the same '*Ooooooh*' you make when you're in third grade and your friend has a crush on someone. He passed it to Zelda, who said "*Ooooooh!*" in an identical tone.

The note read:

> *Are you available tonight at six o'clock? If possible I would like to meet. I think I can provide some clarity, and I hope to put your mind at ease.*
>
> *I have arranged to hold the table until ten. My apologies for the inconvenience and short notice.*

It was signed:

Ezra Fontaine

14 WATER IS FINE

Tony was dressed way too casually.

He had once again made the mistake of trusting Goff, who he'd impulsively called to consult. Goff had reassured him that *of course* there was no dress code, then called him a private car to take him downtown to boot. Tony was actually feeling more warmly towards his cousin... until he stepped out of the car, onto the sidewalk, and saw a couple in a tux and furs step out of their car at the same moment.

The couple gave him a slightly bewildered look, then held their gold-plated cards up to the smiling doorman, who waved them inside.

Tony — dressed in god damn jeans and a polo shirt — expected the doorman to take one look at him and call security, golden ticket or no.

But when he wordlessly lifted his 'ADMIT ONE,' the man gave him the exact same smile of welcome, and the doors parted.

The external facade of the building had been shockingly plain, looking gray and very old, like its roof for *sure* hosted a whole metropolis of pigeons. Inside, however, was a shock of color and textures.

Just *one* color.

Red.

Almost all of the walls, the ceilings, the floors, the furniture, was some shade of red. Walking into the entry parlor was like stepping into a gigantic mouth. It was... kind of horny? If bordering-on-cannibalistic could be horny. It made Tony think of blowjobs. But then again, when wasn't Tony thinking about blowjobs?

The formally dressed couple were already being led away down a hall — down deeper into the gullet of the club — and Tony stood there alone before the hostess desk.

"I'm meeting a friend," he said, trying to project confidence. He held out the card, let her take it, and then hooked his thumbs in his belt loops. Confidence. Swagger. Relaxed. Confidence.

"What's your friend's name?" asked the hostess. She was pretty but not made up, looking more like a secretary in an office than someone who manned the front desk at an exclusive club. She smiled, too, her air just as easy and carefree-friendly as the doorman's had been.

'Friend's name' galled Tony somewhat, the dragon inside of him protesting that this was the name of his *subject*, his *slave*, but Tony shut the dragon the fuck up and said, "Ezra Fontaine."

"Of course!" she said, her customer service smile blooming into something more genuine. "We love Ezra. I was so pleased to see him put down another name."

'We love Ezra'?

Tony blinked a few times, unable to think of anything to say or any way to question what she meant. *'So pleased to see him put down another name.'* Tony had the sudden mental image of Fontaine in the corner of a bar, under blue light, nursing a cocktail all by his lonesome.

"If you'll follow me," she said, putting aside her things and heading down the hall.

She was surprisingly speedy, hard to keep up with even on his long legs. Tony barely got a chance to glance into the rooms they passed by. He caught flashes of what looked like card rooms, a lounge populated by ferns, a line of cage dancers. Each door they passed by bubbled with conversation, or music, or both.

He saw tux after tux, gown after gown.

He was absolutely the *only* person wearing jeans.

But the hostess didn't seem to find anything amiss about him. She was nothing but professional and courteous, maintaining the level facade even when they passed a room where a *peacock* stood in the doorway. It blared at them, one high, petulant squawk that made Tony jump a foot.

By the time they made it through to the end of the labyrinth, Tony was almost too disoriented by his surroundings to worry about his clothes or about meeting Fontaine.

That was, until they passed into a large chamber, full of strange clusters of tables which were half-hidden behind partitions of red silk. There came murmurs of conversation from each cluster, and each fell silent as the two of them passed.

Tony got the feeling that *these* guests were not here for the entertainment.

His spine prickled, but the hostess cheerfully guided him through the odd, red-silk garden and to a wide, curtained doorway.

Beyond that was another curtained doorway, and another, and Tony was starting to feel annoyed, and threw open another set of curtains—

And there sat Fontaine.

A high-backed, semi-circle of a sofa lined the walls of a tiny chamber, which was really more niche than room. The sleek sofa made up a booth, with a round table at the center of it. Not a niche, actually — a nook. A nice, intimate little dining nook.

Fontaine was not wearing a tux.

In fact, he was dressed nowhere near as sharply as Tony was accustomed to seeing him in. No cufflinks, no diamond timepiece. No *tie* even. He wore simply a light jacket, gray, over a white button-up.

It was... a good look. Eatable. Not that he wasn't ever *not* eatable, but in the more casual clothes he looked more comfortable, more... accessible. Lived-in. His typical suits were boxy. They *accessorized* the man, they left almost everything to the imagination. These duds... well, they were a touch more form fitting.

And Tony could not deny the strong visual impression of a general out of his armor.

"Gina?"

The sound of Fontaine's voice made Tony's gut plunge and his mouth go dry, but Fontaine was only talking to the hostess. He was speaking to her... politely?

"Another of these," he said, tapping the rim of an almost-empty cocktail glass. "And whatever he wants."

He didn't look at Tony. He made eye contact with Gina, and he was not an arrogant dick — though nor was he overly friendly. He was... neutral. *Almost* kind. Kind in a very dry, *plain* way. Very difficult to read.

"Of course," said Gina. To Tony, she asked, "Would you like to see our specialty cocktail menu? Or I can bring you the wine list."

It occurred to Tony that no one had carded him at the front door.

Was she going to card him now?

Tony passed easily for late twenties and had never gotten more than a glance at his fake ID, never had a problem getting into clubs or bars. He doubted it would be a problem here.

But the idea of being carded *in front of Fontaine* was an intolerable one. Like— Like — like getting your temperature taken rectally on a first date.

Absolutely not.

"Water is fine," he said, like a god damn moron, slipping into the booth.

His words echoed in his head.

Water is fine... Water is fine...

"Great," said the hostess. "I'll get that out in a minute."

She parted the curtain and left.

And there they sat.

Fontaine didn't immediately speak, and Tony sure wasn't going to be the one to break the silence.

Fontaine's note flashed back in his head. *'I think I can provide some clarity.'*

Clarity about what?

Fontaine had two fingers around the stem of his almost-empty cocktail glass, and he put just the tiniest bit of momentum into it, just enough to slowly swirl the dregs. A curl of something — Orange peel? — floated, moved in small circles.

And then he broke the silence.

Leaving the glass, he reached to the side and produced a bag from under the table — Tony's big black workout bag.

The bag of tricks.

"Your property," said Fontaine.

He didn't try to hand it over, simply put it within reach.

'Your property.'

Something about the way Fontaine said the words drew Tony's attention, distracted him from the anxiety-sweat and endless circling thoughts of what the fuck was happening.

He looked into Fontaine's face.

And Fontaine didn't exactly avoid Tony's gaze... but dropped his own.

Fontaine *lowered his gaze*.

This strange attitude of his, Tony realized, was not really so strange and opaque.

It was *submissive*.

Respectful.

It even bordered on apologetic.

Tony remembered the line from the note: 'My apologies for the inconvenience and short notice.'

"I have this for you, as well," said Fontaine, and produced and pushed over a folder.

Tony paused, then took and opened it, scanning the sheaf of papers inside. He saw what looked like... medical information? Test results?

"That's up to date as of three months ago," said Fontaine. "And there's been no one since then."

Tony blinked. He looked at the papers again. He recognized a few words in a sweep: gonorrhea, chlamydia, syphilis. Negative, negative, negative.

And he recalled Fontaine's note.

'I hope to put your mind at ease.'

He realized. And realized.

Realization after realization smashed together like blocks, building up into a skyrocketing tower of comprehension.

Fontaine was not acting aloof and disconnected, he was *projecting submission.*

The swirling of his glass had not been boredom or restlessness, but *nerves.*

And he had not reacted strangely to Tony's *kiss* in the gym shower, but to the fact that Tony had used a toy on him. Had fingered him. Had come *on* him, but not *in* him.

Had not *fucked* him.

And he had brought proof — actual, tangible, medical *proof* — that his body was safe for fucking. Ready.

Available.

Tony's head felt like a balloon full of cool air. Giddy and floating.

And then fucking *Gina* returned, juggling Fontaine's cocktail, a glass, and a pitcher of ice water.

"Here you are," she said, saying absolutely nothing about the huge, suspicious black gym bag which had appeared on the table. "Anything else you need?"

"Just some privacy, thank you," said Fontaine, polite and no more.

Gina got the hint — which wasn't really a hint — and got on her way.

The curtains fell shut.

Tony put down the folder.

He looked at Fontaine — Ezra *fucking* Fontaine — who did not look back at him, who did not raise his eyes.

Fontaine reached out abruptly for his glass and took a drink.

As if he had needed the liquid courage, he pushed ahead then.

"I don't mean to demand anything," said Fontaine. His voice was quiet, but sure. "I'm not trying to be presumptuous. However, at my age... I can't afford an unofficial arrangement."

'At my age.'

'Unofficial arrangement.'

Fontaine paused, then went on.

"My home," he said, "is furnished for the lifestyle."

'Furnished for the lifestyle.'

Tony envisioned a bed's headboard with chains welded to it. With a crate built into the raised bedframe.

He could feel the Dragon awaking inside of him, coming alive with a purr and a nonchalant 'but of *course*,' that all of this had turned out to be the case. That Fontaine had really been panting for him and had scrambled together this info to prove himself worthy of fucking. To *plead* for it.

But of *course*.

"The signatures..." Fontaine paused for a moment, and Tony remembered them.

The lines streaking down Fontaine's back.

The mark of all the other men who had owned him.

Tony could see the baggage in Fontaine's face, now that he knew how to look for it. The memory of those men weighing heavy on him. '*At my age.*' Spoken as if he knew he were spoiled goods, past his prime. As if his age wasn't one of the top three reasons Tony was drooling, slavering, *panting* after him.

"They're from the past," said Fontaine.

The past.

He said 'past' as if it were a vile word. He clasped his glass's stem again and slowly, gently swirled his drink while gazing into it.

Was he thinking of his past?

Tony thought of those half-removed signatures. Of the more brazen tattoos.

SLUTHOLE. COCKWHORE. FUCKTOY.

Suddenly Fontaine seemed to gather himself, and he raised his gray-green eyes, and asked, "Is that an obstacle for you?"

And Fontaine hung there.

Up in the air.

Up for grabs.

And Tony could *feel it*.

His fingers, talons.

His eyes piercing, golden.

Sharp teeth. Long, cunning tail. Enormous, powerful wings.

He smiled, sat back, took a sip of his water.

"It's not an obstacle for me," he said simply.

Tony put down his glass, made an imperious gesture at Fontaine and his white shirt, gray jacket.

"Take that shit off," he said.

15 EIGHT AND A QUARTER

Fontaine undressed.

He had clearly been hoping for this outcome, and came prepared.

He wore no underwear... but he was not naked.

Instead, he was draped in delicate chain lingerie.

Intricate. Exquisitely crafted, probably incalculably expensive. The sheer extravagance seemed as if he were trying to make up for his referenced age and well use by other men, by covering himself in gilt.

The barbells in his nipples had been swapped out for rings, and from those rings were connected twin chains, which ran up and hooked onto a slim collar, one which had been covered by his buttoned-up shirt.

Another slender set of chains ran from his nipples to his pierced navel. Clipped on.

Another, single chain was clipped to that.

It dangled loose as Fontaine stripped, but when all his clothes fell away, he reached for it. Took it in hand. Reached down and clipped it to the ring pierced through the head of his cock.

Tony's groin *throbbed*.

He imagined Fontaine dressing in the mirror back home. *Planning* this.

Stiffening but not yet hard, Fontaine's cock was *held up* by the chain, by its ring, like a bull led by the nose.

And that wasn't all.

A loose loop of chain encircled his waist, from there connecting to a twin set of loops around his thigh, like a metallic garter belt.

And from that loop encircling his waist dangled dozens of extremely thin, light chains, which hung shimmering. Rippling. A short *skirt* of chain link which barely reached midthigh — and which, of course, parted curtainlike so that nothing at all was *hidden,* only accentuated, flirting with the *idea* of hiding as in some burlesque.

And it was all.

It was all.

It was all fucking *silver*.

Fontaine skimmed his fingers over the getup, lightly checking that all was in place, and then looked at Tony with a wary flicker in his gray-green eyes. A vulnerability. Would his Master like it? Would he think it was absurd? Would he—

Tony reached out and grabbed him by the ass, fingers gliding under the whispering silver of the 'skirt' to haul the powerfully built, hunk-of-muscle older man onto his lap. Groping his thighs. Greedily feeling up his back. Leaning forward to suck into his mouth one gleaming, pierced nipple — a glistening locus of silver and diamond and twinging, sensitive flesh on the pectoral's rounded peak.

Caught off guard, Fontaine let out an undefended sound, something like an "*Oh*," but without the full shape of a word.

Tony mouthed him, sucked the twitching point hard between his lips, felt Fontaine's body hitch on top of him.

And thought he might lose his mind.

His cock throbbed like something poisoned. He needed, he *needed* to have his silver fox, his beautiful silver slave, his obsession, split and panting on his cock, bouncing against him.

He raced his hands over the muscular curves of Fontaine's ass, down, back, spreading, seeking with his fingertips.

He found the hard metal of a plug's base.

Impulsively he fitted his fingertips around the edges, hooked them, and applied pressure. Pulling.

Fontaine gasped. His fingers squeezed Tony's biceps.

Tony could feel the size of the plug hidden inside of him. The *weight*.

He realized that Fontaine had taken mental note of his size... and come prepared.

"Do it," said Fontaine hoarsely. His voice strained to stay quiet, mindful of the club patrons not far from earshot. But he urged Tony on, "Do it," not so much encouraging as *begging*, low in his throat, arching his back and hitching his ass up. Offering. Submitting. Wanton. *Worm*.

Tony adjusted his grip tighter and applied firm, steady pressure. *Pulling*. Twisting, rotating.

The body of the plug finally yielded — thick, several inches at its widest point. And it was at that widest point that Tony paused. He gripped the plug carefully — not pulling it out, not letting it slip back inside.

Instead, he let that wide, *stretching* point work on Fontaine's entrance. Feeling the way his body clenched at it. Feeling the way he shuddered. And feeling the hot, rough air of Fontaine's breath on his face.

Tony worked the widest point back, forth. Yielding to a shallower section... then pushing forward once more, challenging Fontaine to spread for him.

Fontaine submitted to every push and shove. Exhaled. Inhaled. His thighs quivered on top of Tony's.

And finally Tony pulled it out.

Pulled it out and immediately, greedily sank his fingers into that warm entrance before it could snug itself tight again.

So fucking... *soft*. Soft, and warm, and silky-slick with remnant lube from the plug, and clenching down on his fingers with deliciously tight promise.

He swirled his fingers, twisted, and plunged them in deep, to the last knuckle.

"Ready to serve your Master properly?"

His words came out whispered against Fontaine's pierced nipple. Followed by a soft, wet suck.

Fontaine's "Yes," came out in a deep gulp, sounding involuntary.

"Get the lube," said Tony. "Ride me."

It was the absolute most he could manage without his voice coming out in a horny-unto-death wheeze.

Fontaine obeyed, sliding off his lap and going for the bag, and Tony sat back with tenting pants and a dizzy head. He wiped the lube from his fingers with a napkin, and realized they were *trembling* from excitement.

Screaming internally at his lack of control — but unable to really blame himself, because *look* what the fuck Fontaine was *wearing* — he put his hands behind his head and went for an appearance of lazy arrogance.

"Other way," he said, when Fontaine went to straddle his lap again. He jerked his chin — all severe half-scowl, 'don't waste my time' — and Fontaine obeyed the direction, facing away from him.

He couldn't let Fontaine see his face for this.

He couldn't even look as Fontaine unzipped him, eased his pants down. Couldn't look as Fontaine braced himself on the table and sat carefully back. One hand wiping Tony Jr. slick, holding him steady.

If Tony had looked, he probably would have busted in seconds.

He shut his eyes at the first sensation of, *god*, the head of his cock nestling against the warm divot.

The sensation of lube, slick and welcoming. The gliding the head of his dick back and forth, rubbing that divot, and then easing into place. Still holding steady the shaft.

Fontaine bore down with his hips and carefully, *smoothly* took the head.

Smooth... but *tight*.

The grip made Tony's head spin.

There should have been more lube, more time; the *tightness* immediately brought to mind a hundred memories of a hundred whining voices, saying 'Tony, it's too much!'

But Fontaine sank down onto the dizzying size with a soft, helpless sound.

A sound of desire.

Tony could *feel* the pain in the way Fontaine's body squeezed, how his dick nearly tried to pop out, but Fontaine did not retreat, did not hesitate... only rocked his body lightly up and down, tormenting his entrance with the thickest point of the head.

Working himself open.

Tony finally couldn't resist.

He opened his eyes to look down at it.

At his personal monster, standing up thick and angry.

At Fontaine's muscular ass, poised atop it.

At the point where the bell of his cockhead disappeared, reappeared, disappeared again. Bobbing.

And then there was a pause — and then a sudden *glide* of skin.

Fontaine's hips sank down by several inches, a smooth enveloping, taking, and Tony saw his monster vanish halfway into that *perfectly shaped* muscle peach of an ass.

He pressed his lips white-tight together so he didn't groan.

Fontaine groaned.

Softly.

Painfully.

His hands braced on the table, he worked himself up and down, caressing the several inches of dick he'd managed to take. Caressing his own insides.

The groan said that it hurt. It was too much. Too thick, too fast.

But the shudder that ran through his body, and the way his hips began to bob more vigorously, said that *oh god*, he wanted it.

His head fell back, and it was unmistakable:

A pleasure that defied physics and all sense of personal safety.

Fontaine's hips and thighs were straining for it, his sides almost heaving with the effort to ride such a beast.

Without thinking, Tony reached for him.

Without thinking he cupped Fontaine's waist, guided him forward, set his elbows to rest on the table. Without thinking, Tony sat up. Stood up. Sent Fontaine with a sharp gasp, with one sharp moan — of pain, and surprise, and then a dark gratification — bending over, forehead and silver hair almost touching the tabletop.

Tony gave it to him from behind. Smoothly — almost gently.

Almost.

There was only so much you could do with his kind of girth.

While Fontaine bent over, white-knuckling on the tabletop, Tony worked the first three or four inches back and forth inside of him, *trying* to be gentle.

He reached around, slid his hands up to cup Fontaine's round pecs, and began to rub and squeeze them. Soothingly.

Yep. Soothingly.

It was definitely about soothing Fontaine, and not about fulfilling the fantasy that had lived in his head for what felt like eternities.

Grasping those big muscly puppies. *Filling* his palms — and he had big fucking palms, okay — with them, taking a handful each of his long-imagined bliss and *massaging*.

Tony was so caught up in rubbing, touching, that he didn't even realize at first that Fontaine had begun to gasp.

Softly. Then not so softly.

Tony closed thumb and forefinger around one nipple, made a back and forth 'playing the world's smallest violin' motion, and Fontaine's hands spasmed on the table and he exclaimed wordlessly.

The dragon's impulse — dark, romantic, sadistic — suddenly reared its head.

And impulsively Tony bent over Fontaine's back, took a tight pec-grip in each hand, and sent himself deeper.

Not three or four inches but four, and then five, and then *six*, and five, four, *six*, five, *six*, five, *six*, *six*, *six*.

And rolling Fontaine's nipples *hard*, soft, *hard*, teasing, stroking, hard, *brutal*, hard, soft, *cruel*.

Fontaine responded as if electrocuted — with convulsions. He seized Tony's forearms in a death grip, fingernails burying themselves deep. His body, his muscles went rigid. The arc of *'too much, too much, unbearable'* coursed through him.

But what came out of his mouth was a moan of *pure* pleasure.

So pure it was *obscene*.

Obscene, and involuntary, and *loud*, as Tony's six solid inches drove him hard up against the table. Pulsing, punching, *thick* inside of him. Unbearable. And he moaned.

And then Fontaine actually clamped a hand over his mouth.

Tony paused.

Was that a sign? Too much? As in — *really* too much?

"I'm sorry," Fontaine managed. He was panting almost too hard to speak.

"Too much?" Tony eased back. Four inches. Was that all right? Three?

"No," moaned Fontaine again, this time in desperation. He *pushed* his hips back, bracing himself again on the table, and took back all six inches with a glad shuddering. *Painful,* but glad. "I can take it, Master. I can keep quiet."

Tony had yet another realization.

Fontaine thought that *he* wanted discretion.

Fontaine thought that *he*, Anton Cargill, so-so greasemonkey and expert DILF hunter, didn't want the people sitting nearby to know he was having *sex*.

Tony almost let out a truly crazed, man-with-his-finger-on-the-big-red-button cackle.

He ran his hands down from Fontaine's chest to his groin, blind but unerringly catching the man's cock near-delicately in one hand, grasping his balls hard-and-tight in the other.

"I don't want you to keep quiet," said the dragon.

"I want you to *come*."

He gave Fontaine seven inches.

Bending him *flat* over the table. Urgently stroking his hard, hard, twitchy, *needy* cock. Squeezing his balls. Pulling them. *Punishing* them. Stroking him. *Fucking* him.

Seven inches.

Six, five, six, *seven.*

Seven. Seven. Seven.

Seven and a quarter, three, four, *seven*.

Fontaine let his mouth hang open and hid nothing.

His noises drove Tony *rabid*.

He had never heard anyone get fucked so *earnestly*, with such clarity of want in their voice, utterly wordless but utterly unmistakable. Fontaine's pain was obvious; pain was the bedrock of each yelping, bounding, transcendent moan. And yet the *ecstasy*. The sound of absolute want. Need. Begging for it. Affirming each brutal stroke.

Tony lost his mind.

He buried his face in the back of Fontaine's neck and drooled like an idiot, completely lost. Aware only of the good, hot plunging between the older man's legs. The intense clutch of his body. Sheer nutty bliss.

It was the dragon who at some point tossed Fontaine over, pulling out long enough to lay him down upon the couch, on his back, silver chain sparkling and falling all about his waist and his thighs, and it was the dragon who unclipped the chain from Fontaine's pierced cock and bent to suck him down deep.

Fontaine was jerking under him, making spastic sounds. A new variant on pain and pleasure. He had already come; his cock was on fire with nerves, far too sensitive for Tony's rapacious sucking, and yet.

Tony sucked all the more greedily.

He thumped his thumb in against Fontaine's prostate, milking with brutal, artless efficiency, and he got what he wanted. And he swirled it around in his mouth, around the head of Fontaine's cock, swirled, swallowed, and gave one final long, relishing suck.

When he raised his head, Fontaine looked as wrecked as he had the night before lying on the shower floor. No. More wrecked. Nothing but trembles. Twitching, jerking from head to toe. Naked. Eyes wet.

Mouth hanging open, jaw exhausted. Lips wet. Too exhausted to swallow his spit, which was sliding down his cheek.

He gazed at his Master with the glazed eyes of a man half-dead.

"Spread your legs," grated the dragon. His own voice was gone from panting... or maybe it was his real voice coming through at last.

Fontaine's half-dead eyes gleamed.

He spread his wildly-shaking thighs, opened himself up, and let out a low, wanton noise as Tony heaped himself down on top.

Tony wormed his way inside, driving with his hips, spreading Fontaine all over again. The sound of mingled pain and joy, of hot excitement, delirium, puffed against his ear as Fontaine gasped, and groaned, and made lost, pleading sounds that could have been for mercy or for more.

Tony thrust with his whole weight, and heaved all eight and a quarter inches balls deep into Fontaine's well-abused insides.

And Fontaine let out a very soft moan, just beside his ear. Just one word.

The low moan of "*Master.*"

Tony fucked lazily, self indulgently, hardly moving. *Lying* there. Giving Fontaine eight inches. Eight and a quarter. Eight. Eight and a quarter. Eight and a quarter.

With each half-assed stroke, his balls coming home to kiss, to throw themselves against Fontaine's taint.

Grind. Thrust.

Indulge. Relish.

Lizard brain wide awake. No one else at home.

Fontaine breathing "Master, Master," against his ear on each stroke, with the mindless, absent satisfaction of someone who had been waiting eternities to say the words.

Tony finished him kissing.

Mouth full of each other.

His asshole contracting, hips humping pointlessly, cock already buried deep with no place to go.

Fontaine's chain lingerie leaving deep red marks on them both.

Fontaine's pierced cock lay flattened under Tony's belly, a strange and sticky spot of cool metal.

And Fontaine's hands touched his face, trembling-tired, but still exploring. Recalling and memorizing afresh the feel of a Master's kiss.

16 EPILOGUE

Tony was still ninety percent asleep — aloft in one of his Dragon dreams — when he felt the first distant touch of lips on his ankle.

His dream faded gradually as those lips followed their usual path upwards, and he was only seventy percent dreaming when they reached his knee. Only fifty percent when they began creeping up his inner thigh, and only thirty when they brushed his balls with first a tip of the nose... then a soft kiss. And then he hit fifteen percent. Eyelids cracking open.

Tony rolled over onto his stomach, sprawling, to give the beloved worm better access to his assets. He turned his sleepy head on the pillow and faced a striking view: the morning sky, dawning red and gold, pushing purple into the fading black corners.

Royal colors.

The thought rolled over Tony mistily as the last dragon's wingbeat evaporated in his mind, and then he was just a deadbeat greasemonkey once more. Lying on his stomach in a king-sized bed, surrounded by the almost Rococo interior stylings of Ezra Fontaine's bedroom, in a house up on the hills — one with a definitively better view of the city than Tony's borrowed apartment.

Lying with the face of the silver fox himself buried between Tony's asscheeks, tongue lolling along the seam of his taint and fantastically sensitive hole, rimming him awake into another lovely morning.

Tony hiked one leg up — mountain climber style — to better let Fontaine eat him out, propping himself up on one elbow to glance back over his shoulder.

There, under the Egyptian cotton, wormed the shape of the man. At the end of the bed, trailing out from under the sheets, was a long, skinny chain fastened to one of many rings welded into the custom footboard.

Fontaine rustled and repositioned himself under the sheets.

Tony knew what that meant.

He closed his eyes again and sank into bliss as Fontaine pulled his stiffening cock back, between his legs, to suck him from the back.

Life was good.

He stretched out with his hand, felt around on the bedside table — Nope, bottle of lube. Nope, set of handcuff key rings. — until he found his phone and brought it to his face, squinting through the morning's notifications.

Jonah and Zelda had sent him some pics. Them, white water rafting, twin screams of horror and elation on their faces. Jonah's ear, freshly pierced. Both of them, attempting to hold a massive python at some zoo or state fair.

And the usual string of unanswered, missed calls from work. Parents. Zachary Goff.

Tony selected a recent message and put the phone to his ear.

"—if you think you can just walk out on a deal with *me*," came his cousin's voice, sounding unhinged. Ranting. "Then you're stupider than I thought."

Tony tried a different message, slightly older.

Goff's voice, calmer this time. Icily sweet. "—just curious when you're going to stop by the office. The guys I sent by the apartment said you weren't home. Too bad, I had another present for you. All you have to do is call me back, Anton. Don't keep me waiting too long..."

Another message, one of the first he'd left.

"A deal is a deal, Tony." Cool, clipped voice. Goff at his most shrewd. "You've got your pet — you're welcome, by the way. If you want to keep your cozy little apartment, and not end up sleeping in that shitty car again, call me back so we can make this official."

Tony scrubbed at his sleep-sandy eyelids and, squinting down at his phone, managed to hit return call.

He rolled over onto his back and swept away the blankets.

Fontaine looked up at him, and the sight lit a flare of joy and heat in Tony's stomach.

All taut muscle, tousle of brilliant silver hair, those gray-green eyes sharper than ever and fixated on his *Master*.

A perfectly fitted leather collar around his throat.

Tony dragged him up by the collar, hooking one finger in the metal loop and pulling Fontaine onto his lap.

Fontaine straddled him *just so,* thrusting their cocks together and grinding in exactly the way his Master liked.

Tony held the ringing phone between shoulder and ear and reached for the lube.

When Goff picked up, Fontaine was already four inches down and working on a fifth. Hips rising and falling, mouth open, eyes slivered with rapture but still fixed on Tony's face. Tony grabbing ass and enjoying the view.

"Anton," said Goff, his voice utter ice.

"Hey cuz," said Tony brightly. "Hey, so, about the apartment."

A kind of puckered silence on Goff's end, a sour lemon-biting absence of words.

And then Goff asked, teeth audibly clicking together, "What *about* it?"

"I don't need it after all," said Tony. "I got a new place. But hey, thanks for letting me crash."

An even sourer silence.

Tony watched Fontaine take six inches, six and a half, working his way down with eyes now rolling.

"Anton," said Goff. His voice was almost *friendly* now. "Have you thought about what you're doing?"

The answer was no, obviously. Tony had not 'thought' about anything for the past three weeks that did not involve collars, manacles, lube, sucking (dick and/or face), fucking, bondage, or anything tangentially related to getting sloppy with Ezra Fontaine.

"I am not a man you want to make an enemy of," Goff was saying, with the patient, even fond air of someone giving advice to a wayward younger relative. "I am—"

"Turn around," said Tony.

"What?" said Goff, startled.

"Not you," said Tony impatiently, and hung up. He tossed the phone aside and tugged the chain linking Fontaine's nipple rings, making him gasp and refocus on Tony's face. "Come on, up and at 'em."

Fontaines eyes gleamed.

"Yes, Master," he said, husky and *slutty* with it, in a way that had gradually emerged with his growing confidence in the past weeks.

He turned himself around without coming fully off of Tony's dick and, once facing the other direction, began seamlessly to ride again, sinking back down to engulf a good six inches.

Tony ran his hands down Fontaine's back.

He traced the lines of the partly-finished dragon tattoo. Only an outline and basic colors right now, once shaded and fully detailed it would completely annihilate any remnant of the old names, covering Fontaine's entire back with black and gold splendor. And it would be done soon; the artist had cleared his entire schedule for them after hearing the story about Goff. Having a man of many enemies for a cousin had its pros.

The empty eye sockets of the dragon seemed to stare right back at Tony.

Then Fontaine turned his head, glancing over his shoulder, and their gazes fused together.

Tony sat up. The motion pushed him deeper into Fontaine — who only groaned, and took it.

Tony fixed his hands on Fontaine's waist and bit down on his shoulder, already purple from regular encounters with his teeth, then went for the kiss, sealing their lips greedily together while his fingers swarmed into Fontaine's lap.

He took hold of Fontaine's cock — being careful with the fresh frenum piercing — and thrust his final inch-and-a-quarter inside of him.

Fontaine shot between Tony's fingers and over the mess of blankets, body clenching right around him, mouth gasping into his.

Tony had a feeling of being aloft again, just like in his dream. Wings spread. Looking down, surveying his kingdom.

Master of all things.

Enjoy this book? Check out *Claiming the Cleanfreak* for a rougher story also featuring Zachary Goff, about a class A shitheel who becomes obsessed with his coworker's nipple piercings.

For a heads up on future releases, sign up for my newsletter and get a free steamy story, *Checkmate*, about a taboo teacher-student relationship with a sizzling reunion.

You can find early access to new work (as well as exclusive bonus content) on my Patreon.

Thanks for being a reader!

ABOUT THE AUTHOR

Daniel May writes MM romance and erotica with a focus on dark contemporary and the occasional vampire. Originally a lover of sci-fi and fantasy, he turned his sights on the erotic as a joke that went over surprisingly well.

www.danielmayauthor.com

ALSO BY DANIEL MAY

Obsessed With Him series

Claiming the Cleanfreak

Princess

Taste of Ink trilogy

The Taste of Ink

The Guilty Canvas

The Final Stroke

The Hanged Men mafia series

Blood Sports

War Games

Man Hunt

Garden of Fiends vampire series

Crimson Halo

Sleepwalkers

Works on Smashwords

Made in the USA
Monee, IL
21 February 2025